I0654700

Joseph Faulkner

The Life of Philip Henry Sheridan

The Dashing, Brave and Sucessful Soldier

Joseph Faulkner

The Life of Philip Henry Sheridan
The Dashing, Brave and Sucessful Soldier

ISBN/EAN: 9783337135904

Printed in Europe, USA, Canada, Australia, Japan

Cover: Foto ©Raphael Reischuk / pixelio.de

More available books at **www.hansebooks.com**

THE LIFE OF

PHILIP HENRY SHERIDAN

*THE DASHING, BRAVE AND SUCCESSFUL
SOLDIER*

BY
JOSEPH FAULKNER

———————

NEW YORK
HURST & CO., Publishers
122 Nassau Street

———

Copyright, 1888, by HURST & CO.

ARGYLE PRESS,

PRINTING AND BOOKBINDING,

265 & 267 CHERRY ST., N. Y.

THE LIFE OF
GEN. PHILIP HENRY SHERIDAN.

BIRTH AND BOYHOOD.

THIRTY years and more have passed since Brevet Lieut.-Gen. Winfield Scott, from Army Headquar-ters at New York, issued, on the 13th of November, 1857, a retrospective general order, of which the following was a portion :

"VIII. April 28, 1856, Brevet Lieut.-Col. E. J. Steptoe, Ninth Infantry, commanding Companies A, E, F, and I, same regiment, and detachments oi Company E, First Dragoons, and Company I, Third Artillery, in all 200 men, at the Cascades, Washington Territory, repulsed the Indians in their attack on that place. The troops landed under fire, routing and dispersing the enemy at every point, capturing a large number of their mules and destroying all their property.

"Second Lieut. Philip H. Sheridan, Fourth In-fantry, is especially mentioned for his gallantry."

Within ten years from the event thus recorded the young Lieutenant who received this flattering

mention had become the renowned hero of Cedar
Creek and a Major-General in the regular army,
while in due time followed promotion to the grades
of Lieutenant-General and General, with the command of that army from which, alas, death has
now removed him in the fullness of his matured
powers.

The career of Philip Henry Sheridan has a tinge
of romance running through its more brilliant
phases, and is a vivid illustration of the truth that
to the born soldier war is the pledge of renown.
The second son of John and Mary Sheridan, who
had emigrated from County Cavan, Irland, a few
years before his birth, and, after settling in Canada
and Albany had drifted westward to Perry County,
in Southern Ohio, he was born in the little village
of Somerset, in that county, on the 6th of March,
1831. He had two brothers, of whom the younger,
Lieut.-Col. Michael V. Sheridan, has long been
upon the late general's staff. A sister, Mary, was
married, and is no longer living. The elder brother,
John L., has engaged in several employments at
the West.

Somerset was then an exceedingly unpretentious
place of perhaps 1200 inhabitants, and has grown
but little since. It is a coincidence that the three
officers who attained the highest rank in the Union
army were all born in Ohio, and the home of General Sherman was but a few miles from that of General Sheridan. The lad's father, who had obtained
employment in road building, bettered himself, and
eventually took contracts for constructing a part of
the National Road from Cumberland to Terre Haute

and for excavating locks and other portions of the Hocking Valley canal, and for work on the Zanesville and Maysville turnpike. His labor kept him away from Somerset most of the time, and the children were left to be brought up by their mother in their cottage. In later years her illustrious son procured for her a very comfortable home in Somerset, where she lived with John L. and his wife and daughters. There, too, she died, at the age of 87, in June, 1888, during the general's dangerous illness.

Like the other village boys, Philip Sheridan went to the school of the place, and was taught reading, writing, grammar, arithmetic, and geography. Many apocryphal stories have been told of Sheridan's boyhood, one of them making him the driver of a water cart in Zanesville. A water cart in that region would have been indeed a novelty then. A more plausible anecdote tells of his once riding a colt barebacked, when his companions expected to see him thrown off, and sticking to his seat with a grit that marked him in renowned rides of later days.

When about twelve years old, being able to do something toward earning his living, he got a situation in the store of John Talbot, in the village, at wages of $2 a month. After working a while there he changed to the store of David Whitehead, where he received $5 a month. His third place was the store of Henry Dittoe ; and by this time, being considerably older and more useful, he commanded $10 a month. His service for Mr. Dittoe gave a chance, while pushing trade and carrying goods, to see a little of the country beyond the village.

WEST POINT AND PACIFIC.

It happened, when he had arrived at the age of sixteen, that there was a vacancy in the cadetship at West Point belonging to the Congressional district in which Somerset is situated. He had always been fond of reading history and biography, and perhaps more particularly the history of wars. A year or two before, the country had become involved in hostilities with Mexico, and possibly through the years 1846 and 1847 the news of the victories of Taylor and Scott may have given him the desire to lead the life of a soldier. At all events, Congressman Thomas Ritchie, who had the appointment to the vacancy at the Military Academy in his control, knew the active young employé of Dittoe, and the lad ventured to apply to him for the appointment. The answer to his request inclosed a document directing him to report at West Point for examination June 1 of that year, 1848. Devoting all his available time to his studies, he repaired to the Military Academy at the time appointed, and to his great joy succeeded in passing the entrance examinations.

The change thus made in the lad's surroundings and prospective career was as great as it had been sudden. Through the seventeen years of his life he had been accustomed only to his native village and its surroundings, save that during the previous year or more he had occasionally gone, as has been indicated, to Zanesville, about eighteen miles away, or over to Lancaster, General Sherman's birthplace, distant about sixteen miles. The journey through Pennsylvania and the city of New York was itself a revelation, since never until that time had he even ridden upon a railroad. At West Point he found many companions from the city, and some who had been prepared for the Military Academy from childhood up. He was fortunate in having an industrious room-mate during the first six months of the course—Cadet Henry W. Slocum, afterward a distinguished major-general. Slocum helped him a great deal with his algebra, of which subject, as of geometry, he knew nothing before entering the Academy. Cadet Slocum was aiming at a high standing in his class, and did, in fact, graduate No. 7; Cadet Sheridan was devoting himself to the less ambitious, but even more anxious, problem of simply trying not to be "found" deficient at the January examination, which was for him the immediate necessity. Accordingly, after taps, when lights were to be put out, and everybody was to go to bed, these two room-mates were in the habit of hanging a blanket over the window, relighting the lamp, and pursuing their studies. At the examination Slocum went far up toward the head of the class, and Sheridan successfully passed his examination and remained in the Academy.

The years sped away, and acquaintances destined to be renewed under strange circumstances and with curious redistributions of fortune and success were made. In Sheridan's class, which was to graduate in 1852, there were some names that were to become well known. The highest scholar was Col. T. L. Casey of the Engineers; Gen. D. S. Stanley graduated No. 9 ; Jerome L. Bonaparte, No. 11 ; the Confederate Gen. Cosby, No. 17 : Gen. G. L. Hartsuff, No. 19 ; Gen. C. R. Woods, No. 30 ; Gen. A. V. Kautz, No. 36 ; Gen. George Crook, No. 38. There were 43 graduates in this class, but of course more members earlier in the course.

But Philip Sheridan was not to graduate with that class. In the fall of 1851, when he had already begun his last year, which would have closed the following June, he had a quarrel with a fellow-cadet, who was an officer in the corps, and being adjudged guilty of a breach of discipline and good conduct, was punished by suspension for a year. On returning to the Academy he joined the succeeding class, that of 1853. Of this the distinguished James B. McPherson was the first scholar, while Gen. J. M. Schofield, who now succeeds Sheridan in command of the army as senior Major-General, graduated No. 7.   The gallant Sill, killed at Stone River, was No. 3, and Terrell, killed at Perryville, was No. 16 ; Gen. R. O. Tyler was No. 22, and Gen. J. B. Hood No. 44.   Sheridan was No. 34 in a class of 52 members, and, five years after entering the Academy, was graduated July 1, 1853, and appointed a Brevet Second Lieutenant, being assigned to Company D, First Infantry.

Then as now the General Regulations gave a three months' leave of absence to graduated cadets before joining their commands, and when this had expired Lieut. Sheridan reported, Sept. 30, for duty at Newport barracks.   With him were ordered to the same garrison, of his class at West Point, Lieuts. Elmer Otis, First Infantry ; H. H. Walker, Third ;

L. L. Rich, Fifth ; R. R. Ross, Fourth ; W. Craig, Third. Just before Christmas orders were issued from Gen. Scott's headquarters, directing certain officers, including Lieut. Sheridan, to join their companies in Texas, via Corpus Christi, and a few months later, accordingly, found him at Fort Duncan. On the 20th of May he was transferred to Camp La Peña, where he commanded Company A for a time, relieving Capt. Caldwell, then rejoining his own company at Turkey Creek. The winter was passed at Fort Duncan, and while there he learned of his becoming a full Second Lieutenant in Company D, Fourth Infantry.

The Fourth Infantry was then serving on the Pacific, and accordingly in May, 1855, Lieut. Sheridan was ordered to report to Governor's Island, New York Harbor, to prepare for going with recruits to Benicia, in the Department of the Pacific, and thence joining his company. His next journey, therefore, carried him to Fort Columbus, where he remained on duty in June and July, and thence he departed for San Francisco.

The great Northwest was then still little more than a wilderness. The discovery of gold at Sutter's mill, in 1848, had rapidly built up California, and that same year the "County of Oregon," comprising everthing north of California up to the forty-ninth parallel, received a Territorial government, while in March, 1849, Joseph Lane arrived as its first Governor. Only a year or two before Lieutenant Sheridan's arrival the so-called District of Vancouver had been set apart to form Washington Territory, with the Columbia River on the west and the forty-sixth parallel on the east, dividing it from Oregon. The same year that he reached this region gold had been found in the Pend d'Oreille or Clark's River at its junction with the Columbia. Foreseeing the rush which this discovery would produce upon lands still belonging to the red men, the Government strengthened its military forces in the region and kept them alert. Governor Stevens of Oregon, on the 9th of June, 1855, made a treaty at Camp Stevens, now Walla Walla City, with the Cayuses, the Walla Wallas, and the Umatillas for the purchase of about 20,000 square miles of land in the gold-bearing region. Ratification by the Washington Government was required in order to make the treaty valid, but without waiting for that gold-seekers spread all over the ceded land and flocked to the Colville mines. The head chief of the Walla Wallas had been reluctant to sign the treaty, and the greed of the whites in seizing the land long before the stipulated price had been paid for it led to bitter hostilities. This animosity extended to tribes all along the line of the Columbia.

Such was the critical period in the history of the far Northwest when Sheridan arrived on the Pacific coast. The first duty assigned to him was that of escorting a topographical party from Sacramento to the Columbia River, in August and September, 1855. The survey was under charge of Lieutenant Williamson, and the military party was under Lieutenant Gibson, while a detachment of the First Dragoons was under Second Lieutenant J. B. Hood. At the Rocky Hills, known as the Three Sisters, in the lava beds, Lieutenant Sheridan took command

GENERAL SHERIDAN IN THE VALLEY.

in place of Lieutenant Hood, who was relieved for other duty. The region was full of elk and deer, and the officers had opportunity of hunting. Careful scouting, however, was required on account of the troubles with the Indians.

This duty having been performed, Lieutenant Sheridan was still continued on detached service from his infantry company-in order that he might command in an expedition against the Yakimas the same detachment of dragoons which had formed a part of Lieutenant Williamson's escort. The expedition started from Camp Yakima, on the north side of the Columbia, opposite The Dalles. Company C, First Dragoons, scouted ahead through a dangerous pass and came out on a branch of the Yakima. There the troops dismounted and advanced, skirmishing. The Indians retreated and the troops encamped at night on the river. On resuming the march the next morning the Indians fired on Lieutenant Sheridan's advance as it deployed, concealing themselves on the mountain-sides. Little harm, however, was done.

After the close of this expedition, Lieutenant Sheridan remained at Fort Vancouver until the opening of. the spring of 1856 made operations again practicable, when he resumed scouting against the Indians.

In November of the same year the Indians had attacked the blockhouse at the Middle Cascades, and had the inmates badly whipped and in imminent danger of being massacred at any moment. A courier was sent flying away to Vancouver, where Sheridan held the fort at that time, calling for immediate assistance. Sheridan caused an old-fashioned iron cannon to be placed on board a little steamer, and in a remarkably short space of time was steaming away up the Columbia. Arriving at the Cascades, the cannon was put on shore and taken to a position on the bank of the river in range of the beleaguered blockhouse, which was surrounded by yelling savages. In the excitement of the moment the gun was placed near the bank and loaded very heavily. The order was given; a fearful boom, which crashed and re-echoed throughout the mountains, was heard. The cannon kicked over the bluff and went splashing into the Columbia, twenty feet below. The artillery was silenced, and Sheridan stood perplexed. His chagrin was turned to joy as he beheld the savages running with all their speed for the mountains, yelling as only savages could. They had never before heard the report of a cannon, and imagined the judgment day had come. Sheridan won his first victory, saving the lives of those in the blockhouse and probably many others, as one success of the hostiles would have caused a raid down the river. Some of the men said that the Indians did not quit running until they had crossed Snake River, in Idaho. A few years ago the cannon was recovered and taken to Portland, Ore., where it was broken up and cast into more useful form.

For gallantry in an engagement at the Cascades of Columbia, April 26, 1856, he was specially noted in general orders. In May following he took command of the Yokima Reservation, in the coast range of mountains. He then selected a site for a

military post in the Seletz Valley. In the spring of
1857 he was complimented by General Scott for
meritorious conduct in the settlement of difficulties
with the Indians at Yokima Bay. In the same
year he built a post at Yamhill, W. T. During
the following years he was actively engaged against
Indians in the mountain ranges. At Grande Ronde
Indian reservation he was still in command of his
detachment of Company C, First Dragoons, and it
was not until the summer of 1857 that he finally
joined his own regiment, and was attached to Company K, at Fort Yamhill. The post was under
command of Capt. D. A. Russell, afterward a
division commander in Sheridan's Army of the Shenandoah, and killed at Winchester. Lieut. Sheridan was on several occasions in charge of the post
during Capt. Russell's absence. The fatigues and
hardships incidental to such a life hardened him
until he became as tough as a hickory sapling and
hardy as a Northern pine. Friends have heard him
tell of living on grasshoppers for days together—a
light diet which might fitly train a man for the long
cavalry raids which were afterward characteristic of
Sheridan's operations. He once carried his provisions for two weeks in a blanket rolled across his
shoulders.

THE OUTBREAK OF WAR.

And now had come the great struggle which was
to call officers of the regular army to more moment-
ous duties. The steady drift of the country toward

civil war had been watched by the little garrisons on the Pacific coast with straining eyes. One of its earliest effects was felt in the resignation of Southern officers there as elsewhere, following their States as these successfully plunged into the abyss of secession. Promotions began to be rapid in the spring of 1861. The modest wish attributed to Lieut. Sheridan was that he might "get a captaincy out of this thing" before it was over. His wildest dream would hardly have led him to imagine that in so few years he would be raised from the rank of Second Lieutenant to that of Lieutenant-General.

Yet even of the brief time which was to be adequate for his fame, a fourth part was to pass with few laurels for him. Brig.-Gen. E. V. Sumner was in command of the Department of the Pacific in 1861, with R. C. Drum and D. C. Buell successively as Assistant Adjutant-Generals. In June, 1861, Col. Wright, commanding the District of Oregon, was directed by Gen. Sumner to send to San Francisco seved infantry companies of his command. Capt. D. A. Russell's company was one of those selected, and the abandonment of Fort Yamhill being ordered, it proceeded to Portland and San Francisco. Lieut. Sheridan was left behind in command of the post, and there remained until September, 1861. Certainly this was not a promising start for one whose rise was destined to be so rapid and dazzling. The war had been going on for months ; one great battle had been fought, and men like Grant, McClellan, Sherman, and others who were to be named in history with Sheridan were already Brigadier or Major Generals, while he was still hidden away at an obscure place in Oregon. But a change of scene and duty was at hand. He had already received in March his promotion to be First Lieutenant of the Fourth Infantry, and the following May a number of new regiments were organized by direction of the President for the regular army. Among these was the Thirteenth Infantry, and by orders dated the 18th of June, Lieut. Sheridan was commissioned to be Captain in that regiment, to date from May 14. This promotion took him to St. Louis, the headquarters of the regiment thus forming.

We are now at the threshold of the more illustrious portions of the great soldier's career, and if we have lingered long upon its earlier stages, this has been because these are less generally known. Arriving at St. Louis in autumn, his first service was the comparatively peaceful one of presiding over a board for auditing claims. Next he received an appointment on the staff of Gen. S. R. Curtis, who just at the end of the year received a command of about 12,000 men concentrating at Rolla, in Missouri, and called the Army of the Southwest. The duty of Capt. Sheridan was to act as chief Quartermaster and Commissary of this force. This was not a very marked advance toward the work of field-fighting, which was the strong point of Sheridan, and, besides, he had the misfortune, as it may then have appeared, to dissatisfy his commanding officer and to lose his place on his staff, after the ensuing Pea Ridge campaign. As a consequence he was sent to report to the headquarters of Gen. Halleck, who, after the battle of Shiloh, had taken command in

the field in the advance upon Corinth.   It was now
April or May of 1862.   The war had been going on
a year, many great battles having been fought and
many officers having already achieved a national
renown.   But Capt. Sheridan, who was to be
known in the history of the war as one of its greatest fighters and one of those whose specialty was
the command and tactical handling of troops on the
field of battle, had not yet taken part in the small-
est skirmish, and even at Halleck's headquarters
was resuming a Quartermaster's functions.

Then, at last, his fortune changed.   It chanced
that the Governor of Michigan applied to Gen. Halleck to furnish him a regular officer to be Colonel
of the Second Michigan Cavalry.   Gen. Halleck
had served in California while Sheridan was on that
coast, and knew that that the latter had had command of dragoons ; besides, he was at hand and
available for any duty.   He replied that there happened to be at his headquarters, and temporarily on
his staff, a proper officer for his purpose, and on
the 25th of May, 1862, Capt. Sheridan became Colonel of the Second Michigan Cavalry.

His active field career began at once.   He led his
regiment a few days after his appointment to the
occupation of Booneville, Miss., and took part in
the advance upon the enemy from Corinth to Bald-
win, having skirmishes at the latter point, and at
Blackland and Donaldson's Cross-roads.   Then,
put in charge of a cavalry brigade composed of his
own regiment and the Second Iowa, he was directed
by Gen. Rosecrans to station himself at Booneville,
on the Mobile & Ohio Railroad.   There he was

attacked on the 1st of July, the enemy driving back his pickets. The fighting was very sharp, and Col. Sheridan detached a portion of his command under Major R. A. Alger, Second Michigan, to take the Blackland road and attack the enemy in the flank and rear. The following account of the result is in Gen. Sheridan's own words :

" He went off, and I moved from where I was, near my headquarters tent (I had not discouraged the men by taking down my headquarters), out on the line of battle, just west of the railroad track, in the village of Booneville. The fighting was sharp along the line, and the firing of the enemy seemed to show so much numerical strength I had the greatest anxiety to hear from Major Alger. The hour—the time set to hear from him—was up, but there was no cheering, so I ordered the charge on the enemy, which was my part of the arrangement, and just at that moment a locomotive and two platform cars, loaded with bales of hay for the horses of my command, came down the track from the main army in the rear, right into Booneville and just behind the line of battle. As the troops knew I had sent back for reinforcements to help us, I thought if the engineer were made to blow his whistle it would give them encouragement, so I galloped to him and ordered it to be sounded loudly and continuously. The men heard it and believed the reinforcements had arrived, and I have reason to suppose the enemy thought so too. I never heard such wild cheering as occurred on our part. The enemy broke and ran,

not only on the road, but all over the country.   He
was defeated.

"Now, to go back to Major Alger.   He followed
the enemy with his command armed only with
sabres and Colt's six-shooting pistols.   The enemy
was principally on the Blackland road, and the first
thing the Major struck was the Rebel headquarters,
which were captured and taken back to a white
farmhouse in the rear by a small escort under Lieut.
Schuyler of the Second Michigan.   The charge was
continued into the rear of the enemy as far as Major
Alger could go.   He was unable to come through to
me, as the enemy was too strong, nor did he get
near enough for me to hear his cheering, but, singular as it may seem, it was at the same time that I
made the charge in front, and probably was instru-
mental in the defeat of the enemy by my small
force.   The enemy, as I heard afterward by prisoners, thought he was charged by a large force in
front and a large force in rear.   At all events
he broke and ran.

"My whole force, as I have said before, was 827
men, of which Major Alger's command numbered
about 90.   We followed up the enemy rapidly.
Major Alger, finding he could not get through,
turned back the way he had gone, but only about
one-half, or a little less than one-half, returned, and
many of those brave fellows came back on the horses
of their comrades, riding double, many of them
wounded. I remember very well that nearly all had
lost their hats.   Major Alger did not come back,
and for a short time I thought he had been killed,
and his command thought so too, but while in pur

suit of the enemy I had the pleasure and satisfaction of meeting him. He was dismounted by the limbs of a tree and run over by the enemy, without being noticed in their retreat from my charge in front."

This combat is interesting to note as being the first in which Sheridan held an independent command. The following day, July 2, 1861, Gen. Rosecrans issued a complimentary order, which, barring the exaggerations that were common to both sides at that period of the war and were natural in the necessary absence of exact information, will be read with interest:

"GENERAL ORDERS No. 81.—The General commanding announces to his army that on the 1st inst. Col. P. H. Sheridan, Second Michigan Cavalry, with 11 companies of the Second Michigan and 11 companies of the second Iowa, was attacked near Booneville by eight regiments of rebel cavalry under Chalmers, and after an eight hours' fight defeated and drove them back, leaving their dead and wounded on the field.

"The coolness, and determination, and fearless gallantry displayed by Col. Sheridan and the officers and men of his command in this action deserve the thanks and admiration of the army."

Col. Sheridan's appointment as Brigadier-General of volunteers dates from July 1, 1862, which, it will be observed, was the day of this fight at Booneville. His troops had suffered little, if any, loss in

that affair, and it had brought him a high reward
Next he went to Guntown with a flag of truce, then
occupied the town of Ripley, and in a subsequent
reconnoissance at Guntown, in August, captured
several prisoners and 300 animals, following this
with a skirmish near Rienzi.

The autumn of 1863 found Gen. Sheridan still rapidly advancing. He had received the command of a
division in Gilbert's corps of Gen. Buell's Army of
the Ohio, which was resisting Bragg's advance into
Kentucky. In command of this called the Eleventh
Division of the Third Corps, he took part in the
battle of Chaplin's Hills, or Perryville, on the 8th
of October. In this, his first engagement of importance, Sheridan performed good service in covering
the right of McCook's division alone the line of
Doctor's Creek, which flows into Chaplin's River near
Perryville, and distinguished himself for discreet
judgment as well as ability to handle troops. The
army then marched forward to the relief of Nashville, and when its command was transferred from
Buell to Rosecrans, Sheridan's division became
successively known as the Eleventh and the Third
of the Fourteenth Corps and the Third of the
Twentieth.

MURFREESBORO.

It was under Rosecrans that Gen. Sheridan perhaps first gave full evidence of his real genius as
a soldier by his conduct in the great battle of Stone
River, or Murfreesboro. This prolonged and san-

guinary engagement took place on the last day of
the year 1862 and the first two days of 1863. Bragg
was at Murfreesboro in force. The Union army
was drawn up until it reached the west side of
Stone River, the left wing consisting of three
divisions under Crittenden, the centre of two under
Thomas, and the right of three under McCook.
These last were the divisions of Sheridan, Davis,
and Johnson, which were deployed and carried the
line southward across the turnpike that runs from
Murfreesboro to Franklin. The left wing rested
on Stone River. Bragg's forces were also nearly
all upon the west side of that stream except one
division, Breckinridge's, which was on the east
side. Rosecran's disposition was made for the purpose of attacking with the left and centre, while
the right was simply to hold the enemy's left in
check. But it chanced that Bragg also had a plan
for taking the aggressive, and as bold a one as the
plan of Rosecrans, it being that of turning the
Union right and thus seizing Rosecrans's line of
communications with his base at Nashville. Regarded in the light of this purpose, the Union right
was far from well posted. McCook's corps was
placed from right to left in the order of Johnson,
Davis, and Sheridan, and while it was somewhat
faulty in facing too much to the east while it should
have faced more to the south, and was hardly compact enough to resist attack, the right division,
Johnson's, was almost "in the air," having, to be
sure, one brigade drawn back, and so facing as to
partly protect the rear, but still not supported
there. As a consequence, while Rosecrans on the

morning of the great battle jubilantly moved his left across the river with intent to swing it into Murfreesboro, Bragg was diligently pursuing his plan of massing his troops to destroy the Union right. Since his tactics contained the least preliminary marching, the initiative was practically secured by him, and the first warning of Rosecrans that his own plan had failed was the practical overwhelming of Johnson's division. He promptly retracted his steps in order to save his communications by accepting the gage of battle where it had been thrown down. But before he could relieve the hard-pressed right, Davis's division, in its turn uncovered by the overwhelming of Johnson's, had been forced to give way after nobly resisting several impetuous attacks of Cleburne.

Then came the turn of Sheridan. Fortunately he had had time to prepare, and with that intuition which distinguished him on later fields, he rapidly changed front so as to form a line at right angles to his former one, and for two hours fought a splendid defensive battle. His line consisted of the brigades of Sill and Roberts, with Shafer's in reserve. It lay in the edge of a cedar brake. Three batteries swept the approach in front, which was an open cotton-field. The enemy came on exultantly, and was mowed down by a terrible fire from the guns, yet would not go back until within short infantry range, when a tremendous fire from the troops that had been lying in the timber broke up the attack. With soldierly instinct young Sill, Sheridan's former classmate at West Point, charged out of the woods at the head of his brigade across the field, and hastened the enemy's retreat, achieving a splendid success at the heavy cost of his own life. Sheridan then sent the brigade of Col. Roberts to charge into the adjoining woods, where his flank was again threatened. Once more he was compelled to change front, and this time he got his left into close junction with Negley's division of Thomas's command, while drawing in the other two brigades so as to cover the rear of the main line. In that position he again sustained the repeated attacks of the enemy until his troops, some of whom had nearly exhausted their ammunition, were completely overborne. But he had splendidly sustained his part of the conflict. "It was eleven o'clock," says one writer, "when Sheridan's division, with compact ranks and empty cartridge-boxes, debouched from the cedar thickets to the open plain stretching along the Murfreesboro turnpike. He had lost 1796 men, and with the cost of their heroic lives had won three hours, which Rosecrans, to whom he now reported, had been using to the best advantage. "Here is all that are left," said he sadly, as he joined his chief. The severity of the battle may be illustrated by the fact that all three of Sheridan's brigade commanders were killed.

After Sheridan's division had at length been swept back, the struggle still went on fiercely, and the memorable firmness of Thomas there, as afterward at Chickamauga, proved of invaluable service. The day closed with both armies still on the field. The succeeding days witnessed less vigorous fighting, and at last Bragg voluntarily withdrew, leaving

Murfreesboro, the prize contended for, in the hands
of Rosecrans.

The following March, Sheridan was engaged at
Eagleville, capturing trains and provisions, and
pursued Van Dorn from Franklin to Columbia.
When the advance of Rosecrans to Tullahoma took
place in June, Sheridan's division led the advance
and crossed the Cumberland Mountains and the
Tennessee, with combats at Fairfield, Cowan Station, and University, the latter on the mountain
top, in a sort of national celebration of July 4, 1863,
as if in echo of those at Vicksburg and Gettysburg.
He had occupied Winchester the day before.

This fine strategical move, known as the Tullahoma campaign, was followed a few months later
by the advance of Rosecrans to Chattanooga, and
the disastrous battle at Chickamauga, on the 19th
and 20th of September, 1863. The purpose of Rosecrans to attack and rout Bragg before occupying
Chattanooga was unquestionably sound; but the
manner of putting it into execution proved to be a
faulty, and the reinforcement of Bragg by Longstreet from Virginia placed Rosecrans in a plight
which threatened the ruin of his army. But Thomas
again "plucked up drowning honor by the locks,"
and saved the Union army from a great disaster.
Sheridan's division was one of those that suffered
from a misunderstanding of orders and the rupture
of the line at Chickamauga causing the portion of
the army to which he was assigned to be driven
from the field. During the stubborn resistance
which his division offered there, still another of his
brigade commanders, Gen. Lytle, was killed.

But the chagrin thus suffered was brief. When
Thomas received the command of the Army of the
Cumberland, whose retreat to the stronghold of
Chattanooga he had magnificently covered and in-
sured, and when Grant, having assumed command
at that point, undertook to dislodge Bragg from
the heights of Missionary Ridge, in the great battle
of Nov. 25, 1863, Sheridan's command was in the
foremost line ascending the heights. He crossed
the ridge close by Bragg's headquarters, and instead
of halting pushed on a mile beyond, making fresh
captures of artillery and prisoners. Then his tired
troops went into bivouac, but when the full moon
rose bright on the field of victory, at midnight, on
Granger's suggestion Sheridan again advanced as
far as Chickamauga Creek, capturing more prisoners and stores.

After the battle of Chattanooga, Gen. Sheridan
took part in operations in East Tennessee, and in
January, 1864, was engaged at Dandridge. But the
time approached for still larger opportunities for
fame and service. Grant had been made Lieutenant-General, and had transferred the scene of his
immediate operations to Virginia. He needed a
commander of the cavalry corps of the Army of
the Potomac. Halleck asked, "Why not take
Sheridan?" and Grant replied, "The very man!"
Thus a second time Halleck had made a happy suggestion for Sheridan's advancement, and it should
be remembered to his credit.

Transferred to his new duties, Sheridan started
with his cavalry corps on the great Virginia campaign which began at the Rapidan and ended at

Appomattox In the Wilderness campaign he was engaged at Todd's Tavern, on May 5 and 7, and at the Furnaces on the intervening day. A portion of his cavalry occupied and held for a time Spottsylvania Court House. Then he made a great swoop in the rear of the enemy, cutting the Virginia Central and Richmond & Fredericksburg railroads. His troops were engaged successively at Beaver Dam, Yellow Tavern, Meadow Bridges, and in the outskirts of Richmond ; then, a fortnight later, near the end of May, at Hanovertown and Totopotomoy Creek, Hawe's Shop, Metadequin Creek, and Cold Harbor. Early in June he made a long raid to Charlottesville, fighting at Trevillian Station, Mallory's Ford, Tunstall, St. Mary's Church, and Darbytown, returning to the James River June 28, and then was engaged at Lee's Mills.

IN THE SHENANDOAH VALLEY.

THE vigor thus exhibited brought him into high favor with Gen. Grant; and when Early made his famous raid through the Shenandoah Valley to Washington, threatening that city, and then, falling back into the valley, stationed himself there as if to hold it, Grant chose Sheridan as the man to take the command there and drive him out. On the 7th of August Sheridan received the command of the middle military division, with a force composed of a large part of his own cavalry corps under Torbert, the Sixth Corps under Wright, and

CAMP SCENE ON THE PAMUNKEY RIVER, NEGROS COOKING

a portion of the Nineteenth under Emory, with the Eighth, oftener called the Army of West Virginia, under Crook. This was known as the Army of the Shenandoah.

With this force he promptly drove Early back from Winchester to Strasburg, with slight skirmishes at Kernstown and Kabletown. The reinforcement of Early's troops from Lee's army caused Sheridan in turn to withdraw to Harper's Ferry. Sheridan knew, however, that before long a demand would be made for the return of these extra troops to Lee, who needed them. Meanwhile he had, in conformity with orders received from Grant, destroyed all crops and supplies as far as Strasburg. The instructions of Grant had been as follows :

"In pushing up the Shenandoah Valley, as it is expected you will have to go, first or last, it is desirable that nothing should be left to invite the enemy to return. Take all provisions, forage, and stock wanted for the use of your command ; such as can not be consumed, destroy. It is not desirable that buildings should be destroyed—they should rather be protected ; but the people should be informed that so long as an army can subsist among them recurrences of these raids must be expected, and we are determined to stop them at all hazards."

Grant, who had been anxious to force Early back as soon as possible, visited Sheridan to consult with him, but "saw," says his report, "that there were but two words of instruction necessary. Go in!" He added that "the result was such that I have never since deemed it necessary to visit Sheridan before giving him orders." On the 19th of September, having heard, by his spies, of the previous return of a portion of Early's forces at Winchester to Lee, Sheridan crossed the Opequan Creek with his army and vigorously attacked the enemy drawn up in front of Winchester. His line was formed with the Nineteenth Corps on the right and the Sixth on the left, and with Crook's corps in reserve, the cavalry operating on each flank. A fierce open-field battle resulted, during which at one moment Early succeeded in breaking in at the junction of the Sixth and Nineteenth Corps. But the peril was temporary; and when Crook had been brought up, and the cavalry on the right had come into full play, the enemy was driven completely from the field up the turnpike toward Strasburg. Sheridan at once sent his famous dispatch: "We have just sent them whirling through Winchester, and we are after them to-morrow. This army behaved splendidly." The news caused the greatest excitement through the North. Grant ordered 200 guns to be fired in honor of it, and sent this dispatch:

"I congratulate you and the army serving under you for the great victory just achieved. It has been most opportune in point of time and effect. It will open again to the Government and to the public the very important line of road from Baltimore to the Ohio, and also the Chesapeake Canal. Better still, it wipes out much of the stain upon our arms by previous disasters in that locality. May your good work continue, is now the prayer of all loyal men."

President Lincoln also sent a characteristic dispatch :

"Have just heard of your great victory. God bless you all, officers and men. Strongly inclined to come up and see you.   A. LINCOLN."

The Union loss was about 5000 men, of whom 4300 were killed or wounded ; Early's was about 4000, of whom 2000 were prisoners. As his force was much smaller than Sheridan's, the loss fell more irreparably upon him. Sheridan also captured five guns. For this brilliant victory Gen. Sheridan received promotion to be a Brigadier-General in the regular army, and we should have noted before that he had been made Major-General of volunteers for his conduct at the battle of Murfreesboro.

Without pausing to allow his enemy to recover, Sheridan the next day followed him up the turnpike to Strasburg and attacked him on the 23d in his strong works at Fisher's Hill. The place had been deemed almost impregnable, but Sheridan, by a carefully concealed movement, sent Crook's command to turn the enemy's left while the main force attacked in front, and the result was a second overwhelming defeat for Early. Nothing could resist the impetuous attack of the Union troops under Sheridan's direction, and once more the enemy was driven up the valley with a loss of 16 guns and 1300 or 1400 men, while Sheridan lost only about 400. Early wrote to Lee the following account:

"The enemy's immense superiority in cavalry and the inefficiency of the greater part of mine has been the cause of all my disasters. In the affair at Fisher's Hill the cavalry gave way, but it was flanked. This would have been remedied if the troops had remained steady, but a panic seized them at the idea of being flanked, and, without being defeated, they broke, many of them fleeing shamefully. The artillery was not captured by the enemy, but abandoned by the infantry. My troops are very much shattered, the men very much exhausted, and many of them without shoes."

Sheridan continued to follow up Early, until the latter had retreated so far that Sheridan, always wary, no matter how vigorous, determined that he would no longer move away from his base of supplies, especially as irregular forces were operating against his communications. Accordingly he returned, burning the valley as he went down.

"I commenced moving back from Port Republic, Mount Crawford, Bridgewater, and Harrisonburg yesterday morning. The grain and forage in advance of these points had previously been destroyed. In moving back to this point the whole country, from the Blue Ridge to the North Mountain, has been made entirely untenable for a Rebel army. I have destroyed over 2000 barns filled with wheat, hay, and farming implements; over 70 mills filled with flour and wheat; have driven in front of the

army over four herd of stock, and have killed and
issued to the troops not less than 3000 sheep. This
destruction embraces the Luray Valley and Little
Fort Valley, as well as the main valley. A large
number of horses have been obtained, a proper estimate of which I can not now make.

" Lieut. John R. Meigs, my engineer officer, was
murdered beyond Harrisonburg, near Dayton. For
this atrocious act all the houses within an area of
five miles were burned. Since I came into the valley from Harper's Ferry every train, every small
party, and every straggler has been bushwhacked
by people, many of whom have protection papers
from commanders who have been hitherto in the
valley.

"From the vicinity of Harrisonburg over 400
wagon-loads of refugees have been sent back to
Martinsburg. Most of the people were Dunkers,
and had been conscripted. The people here are
getting sick of the war. Heretofore they have had
no reason to complain, because they have been living in great abundance."

Early, however, who had been reinforced, promptly followed with cavalry under Rosser, who had
been sent by Lee to his aid. Thereupon Sheridan
ordered Torbert to halt and " whip the rebel cavalry, or get whipped himself," Torbert chose the
former alternative, and Merritt and Custer, at Tom's
Brook, Oct 9, drove back Lomax and Rosser,
Merritt capturing five guns and Custer six, with
other spoils. Sheridan sent this news to Grant : " I
directed Torbert to attack at daylight this morning

and finish this 'saviour of the valley.' The enemy, after being charged by our gallant cavalry, was broken and ran. They were followed by our men on the jump 26 miles through Mount Jackson and across North Fork of the Shenandoah. I deemed it best to make this delay of one day here and settle this new cavalry general."

Having reached Strasburg, Gen. Sheridan posted his army in a strong position just beyond at Cedar Creek, and then proceeded personally, on Oct. 15, to Washington in response to a request from Secretary Stanton, who wished to consult him. Meanwhile Early, who had followed the Union forces down the valley, determined to attack them in their camp at Cedar Creek. Aided by a heavy fog in the early morning of the 19th, he succeeded in surprising Crook's command, which was the nearest, and by an impetuous attack completely routed it, having fallen upon Thorburn's division while the men were still asleep in their tents. Gen. Wright, who, as senior officer, was in command, instantly made dispositions to repair the disaster, but the falling back of Crook uncovered the Nineteenth Corps, and, despite its utmost exertions, made its position untenable. The Sixth Corps and the cavalry were got rapidly over to the turnpike, and a desperate struggle ensued to hold that road. Getty's division, which was directly on the pike, was especially pressed, but held its position with tenacity, finely supported by the cavalry on the other side of the pike. The Union camps, however, were all in the possession of the enemy, some of whom were plundering them.

At this juncture Sheridan appeared on the scene. He was on his way back from Washington and had passed the night at Winchester. In the morning the noise of the firing, which was heard even at Harper's Ferry, convinced him that a battle was going on. About 9 o'clock he mounted his horse to ride to his camp, and he had got a very little way from the town when a stream of fugitives from the field told him of probable disaster. Putting spurs to his horse he rapidly dashed up the pike to his army, at a distance of $11\frac{1}{2}$ miles from Winchester. As he rode along he called on the fugitives to turn back, and many of them did so. Arriving at the line he was greeted with cheers on every hand, and the news was spread from man to man even where he was not seen.

Sheridan's army still held the turnpike and still largely outnumbered the enemy. He therefore at once prepared to resume the offensive, and having his forces well in hand advanced upon the enemy, whose line was somewhat disordered by the morning's successes, and after a stubborn contest utterly routed it, driving it in the utmost confusion back across Cedar Creek. To such a transformation scene the war perhaps presents no parallel. Early's loss was about 3000 ; the Union troops lost 6704.

This battle, with its dramatic features, at once made Sheridan the hero of the day. Poets sang of his ride from Winchester and painters depicted it. Grant wrote that "turning what had bid fair to be a disaster into glorious victory stamped Sheridan what I always thought him, one of the ablest of generals." President Lincoln sent this dispatch ;

"With great pleasure I tender to you and your brave army the thanks of the nation and my own personal admiration and gratitude for the month's operations in the Shenandoah Valley, and especially for the splendid work of Oct. 19, 1864."

Congress passed a vote of thanks to "Major-Gen. Philip H. Sheridan and to officers and men under his command for the gallantry, military skill, and courage displayed in the brilliant series of victories achieved by them in the Valley of the Shenandoah, and especially for their services at Cedar Run, on the 19th day of October, 1864, which retrieved the fortunes of the day, and thus averted a great disaster." The legislatures of New York, Rhode Island, and other States also thanked him, while the President appointed him a Major-General in the army, "for the personal gallantry, military skill, and just confidence in the courage and patriotism of your troops displayed by you on the 19th day of October at Cedar Run, whereby, under the blessing of Providence, your routed army was reorganized, a great national disaster averted, and a brilliant victory achieved over the Rebels for the third time in a pitched battle within thirty days."

Early fell back to Newmarket, and there remained two weeks. In November he moved down as if to attack Sheridan, but evidently thought better of it. Sheridan destroyed all the barns and crops in Loudoun County, but there were few other operations until spring, and Early went up to Staunton for winter quarters, and then nearly all his

THE "WHITE FLAG" ON THE ROAD TO RICHMOND.

troops were sent back to Lee at Petersburg. The
Sixth Corps had been sent back to Grant.

On the 27th of February Sheridan moved up the
valley with 10,000 cavalry under Merritt, with orders to destroy the Central Railroad and the canal,
to capture Lynchburg if possible, and then to join
Sherman in North Carolina or return to Winchester.
Finding a remnant of Early's command at Waynes-
boro he fell on it and captured nearly the whole of
it, guns, wagons, tents, and stores. Incessant rains
made terrible roads, but he pushed on, and using
his discretion, ended his march by joining Grant at
Petersburg after " destroying the James River and
Kanawha Canal and cutting the Gordonsville &
Lynchburg, Virginia Central and Richmond &
Fredericksburg railroads, and destroying many
railroads, canal and road and river bridges and
trestlework, and capturing and destroying 60 canal-
boats, containing large quantities of Rebel government property, consisting of ordnance and ordnance
stores, clothing, camp and garrison equipage, commissary stores and medical supplies, and destroying
hundreds of army wagons and ambulances, and several factories, warehouses, tanneries, forges, and
workshops, used for the manufacture of and filled
with military supplies of the description above
enumerated, and capturing 18 battle-flags, 1600
prisoners, and 2143 horses and mules."

The course taken by Sheridan was fortunate, for
it brought him into position for the last grand struggle of the war. When Grant, at the close of March,
1865, began the movements which resulted in the
downfall of Petersburg and the capture of Rich-

mond, Sheridan, placed on the left, piloted the way
with his cavalry.   His first march brought him to
Dinwiddie Court House.   The primary aim of Grant
was to break the last remaining railroads open to
Lee in order to cut off his supplies and force him to
surrender. For this purpose the familiar move by the
left was once more resorted to, the Second and Fifth
Corps forming the infantry column, and Sheridan,
with 9000 sabres, making a broader sweep to the
west.   But after the movement had begun, Grant
sent word to Sheridan at Dinwiddie, instead of
raiding upon railroads to "push around the enemy
and get on to his right rear," since, as he said, "I
now feel like ending the matter."   As soon as Lee
detected Grant's purpose he gathered up all available troops from his intrenched line and, placing
them under the command of Pickett and Johnson,
furiously attacked the Fifth Corps at White Oak
Ridge and Sheridan at Dinwiddie.   The point where
the White Oak Road crosses the road from Dinwiddie to the Southside Railroad is called Five
Forks, and this Sheridan had seized.   The first effort of the Confederate attack had been to drive him
out of Five Forks, and his cavalry was sorely
pressed ; but, thanks to his tactical skill, he got
them in hand on the retreat and placed them safely
behind the intrenchments at Dinwiddie.

It at once became of the highest importance to
recapture Five Forks, from which by marching a
short distance over the Ford road the Southside
Railroad could be reached.   Lee, recognizing also
the importance of this place, had already concen-
trated there the divisions of Pickett and Johnson,

with the brigades of Wilcox and Wise. Grant, on his part, sent to the aid of Sheridan the Fifth Corps, and placed it under his command. Accordingly Sheridan, on the 1st of April, the day after his repulse, began to carry out his plan of battle, which was to drive the enemy well within the works at Five Forks with cavalry, making at the same time a heavy demonstration against his right, and then, behind this thick screen of cavalry skirmishers, to secretly move the infantry corps across to a point where it could strike and turn the enemy's left. At the same time, with that unvarying caution which was as striking a trait as his vigor, he detached a column of cavalry, under Mackenzie, to protect what would become his own right and rear when his line was formed, and this officer, in fact, in executing that duty, found a body of the enemy, which he drove back to Petersburg.

Everything being ready, the infantry was moved by a left wheel, with Ayres's division as the pivot and Crawford's, supported by Griffin, as the wheeling flank. As Sheridan had calculated, it overlapped the Confederate line of parapets, and after a sharp attack, which for a time was left a little doubtful by the disjoining of the infantry divisions, exposing them to a heavy flank fire from the breastworks, the entire position was splendidly carried. The enemy broke and ran, pursued for miles along the White Oak road by Merritt and Mackenzie, and leaving several thousand prisoners and four guns, with many colors, in the hands of Sheridan, whose loss was less than a thousand men, the greater part of this being in the Fifth Corps.

The overthrow of Lee's right by Sheridan at Five
Forks, followed immediately by the carrying of all
the outer line of the Petersburg intrenchments,
made the instant abandonment of Richmond im-
perative. The only line of retreat that promised
success was that of the Appomattox River. The
day after the battle of Five Forks Sheridan moved
a few miles over to the Southside Railroad, striking
it at Ford's Station, and that night Lee's lines at
Petersburg and Richmond were virtually abandoned, while the next morning the blowing up of
the Confederate iron-clads and the firing of the
tobacco warehouses by Ewell's rear guard gave a
token to the Union troops of what was going on.
Then began a race for life, Lee retreating on the
north side of the Appomatox and Grant pursuing
on the south side. The railroad from Richmond
to Danville crosses the Southside Railroad running
west from Petersburg at Burkesville Junction,
which accordingly became a strategic point of
supreme importance. Lee marched directly upon
it, but was pressed to halt for a day at Amelia
Court House until he could get rations and forage,
since supplies which he had ordered to be kept
there had by mistake been carried on to Richmond,
where they perished in the flames. He had reached
Amelia Court House on the morning of April 4,
and Sheridan the same afternoon planted his cavalry, the Fifth Corps, directly across the railroad at
Jetersville, seven miles beyond, being thus between
Lee and Burkesville. The next day Meade came
up to Jetersville with the Second and Sixth Corps,
and meanwhile that morning Sheridan sent a cav-

alry force under Davies still further west, to Paine's Cross-roads, where it defeated a Confederate force and captured many wagons, five guns, and some prisoners.

Seeing his path southwestward to Burkesville blocked, Lee on the night of the 5th moved westward toward Farmville, intending there to recross the Appomattox and reach Lynchburg. At once the Union army was directed on a parallel route from Jetersville, Sheridan leading with the cavalry, the Fifth Corps having been returned to Meade He struck the enemy first near Deatonsville, just north of Jetersville, and gave orders which contemplated successive attacks by divisions along the retreating column, thus forcing it to halt and defend itself. At Sailor's Creek, near Farmville, he struck the enemy again and captured 400 wagons, 16 guns, and many prisoners, and then he ordered a mounted charge of Stagg's brigade in order to detain Ewell's corps until the Union infantry could come up. The Sixth and Second Corps accordingly were engaged in a hot fight, the former in front of Ewell, the latter in his rear, and Sheridan on the flank, the result being the rout of the corps, which was the same one that Sheridan had defeated in the Shenandoah Valley. Thousands of prisoners were captured. At Farmville, the next day, Sheridan again attacked the enemy, capturing prisoners and guns, and at last, on April 9, all was over with the surrender at Appomattox.

SINCE WAR TIMES.

WHEN Lee had surrendered, Sheridan was hurried with a cavalry and infantry force into North Carolina, to Sherman, but was recalled on Johnston's capitulation to the latter. Next he received command of the forces west of the Mississippi, where Gen. Kirby Smith threatened to continue hostilities, but that duty also was quickly ended by Smith's surrender. Then he had charge of the military division of the Southwest, or of the Gulf, and also of the corps of observation established on the Rio Grande to watch the war in Mexico that resulted in the downfall and death of Maximilian. Ensuing political troubles and riots in New Orleans caused much criticism upon him, but the course he took there received the sanction of Gen. Grant. From the Southwest he was transferred to the Department of the Missouri, Sept. 12, 1867, and conducted the campaign against hostile Indians in the winter of 1868-9, resulting in their defeat and surrender.

When Gen. Grant was made President, March 4, 1869, Lieut.-Gen. Sherman was promoted to be General in his stead, and Major-Gen. Sheridan to be Lieutenant-General, the law providing that these two grades of General and Lieutenant-General should cease to exist respectively with these incumbents. The new Lieutenant-General received command of the Military Division in Missouri, with headquarters in Chicago, and afterwards made a visit to Europe. During the Franco-Prussian war of 1870 he was a guest at the headquarters of the King of Prussia and present at the battles of Gravelotte, Beaumont, and Sedan, and afterwards at the headquarters of the German armies at Versailles, witnessing many engagements around Paris during the siege of that city.

The following letter was sent to Gen. Grant by Sheridan, and well illustrates his keen military criticism, and also the terse, clear, and picturesque style of his correspondence :

REIMS, FRANCE, Sept. 13, 1870.

MY DEAR GEN. GRANT : The capture of the Emperor Napoleon and McMahon's army at Sedan on the 1st of September has thrown France into a chaos which even embarrasses the Prussian authorities. It seems to a quiet observer as though Prussia had done too much. Whom to negotiate with ? whom to hold responsible in the final settlement ? are becoming grave questions, and one can not see what will be the result. I was present at the battles of Beaumont, Gravelotte and Sedan, and have had my imagination clipped, in seeing these battles, of many of the errors it had run into in its conceptions of what might be expected of the trained troops of Europe.

There was about the same percentage of sneaks, or runaways, and the general conditions of the battles were about the same as our own. One thing was especially noticeable—the scattered condition of the men in going into battle and their scattered condition while engaged. At Gravelotte, Beaumont and Sedan the men engaged on both sides were so scattered that it looked like thousands of men engaged in a deadly skirmish without any regard to lines or formation.   These battles were of this style of fighting, commencing at long range, and might be called progressive fighting, closing at night by the French always giving up their position, or being driven from it in this way by the Prussians.   The latter had their own strategy up to the Moselle, and it was good and successful.   After that river was reached the French made the strategy for the Prussians, and it was more successful than their own.   The Prussian soldiers are very good, brave fellows, all young, scarcely a man over twenty-seven in the first levies.   They had gone into each battle with the determination to win.   It is especially noticeable also that the Prussians have attacked the French wherever they have found them, let the numbers be great or small, and so far as I have been able to see, though the grand tactics of bringing on the engagement have been good, yet the battles have been won by the good, square fighting of the men and junior officers.   It is true the Prussians have been two to one except in one of the battles before Metz, that of the 16th of August; still the French have had the advantage of very strong positions.

Generally speaking, the French soldiers have not fought well.   It may be because the poor fellows had been discouraged by the trap into which their commander had led them, but I must confess to having seen some of the "tallest" running at Sedan I have ever witnessed, especially on the left of the French position—all attempts to make the men stand seemed to be unavailing.   So disgraceful was this that it caused the French cavalry to make three or four gallant but foolish charges, as if it

EXPLOSION OF TORPEDOES LEFT BY THE CONFEDERATES AT YORKTOWN, VA.

were to show that there was at least some manhood left in a mounted French soldier.

I am disgusted ; all my boyhood's fancies of the soldiers of the great Napoleon have been dissipated ; or else the soldiers of the " Little Corporal" have lost their *élan* in the pampered parade soldiers of the " Man of Destiny."

The Prussians will settle, I think, by making the line of the Moselle the German line, taking in Metz and Strasburg, and the expenses of the war.

I have been most kindly received by the King and Count Bismarck and all the officers at the headquarters of the Prussian army ; have seen much of great interest, and especially have been able to observe the difference between European battles and those of our own country. I have not found the difference very great, but that difference is to the credit of our own country. There is nothing to be learned here professionally, and it is a satisfaction to learn that such is the case. There is much, however, which Europeans could learn from us—the use of rifle-pits—the use of cavalry, which they do not use well ; for instance, there is a line of communication from here to Germany exposed to the whole of the south of France, with scarcely a soldier on the whole line, and it has never been touched. There are a hundred things in which they are behind us. The staff departments are poorly organized; the quartermaster's department very wretched, etc. Very respectfully, your obedient servant,

P. H. SHERIDAN, Lieutenant-General.

P. S.—We go to-morrow with the headquarters of the King to a point about twenty miles from Paris.   P. H. S.

Another step in his career remained, and this he took in receiving the command of the army when Gen. Sherman was retired under the law, as having reached the age of 64. This retirement occurred Feb. 8, 1884, but Gen. Sheridan removed to Washington and assumed his duties the autumn previous, as Gen. Sherman desired to anticipate the actual date. This command Lieut-Gen. Sheridan continued to exercise actively until the occurrence of the illness which resulted in his death at Nonquitt, Mass., Aug. 5, 1888. During his last illness the Senate passed a bill to make him a full General, and the House concurred June 1, the President signing the bill the same day and sending in his nomination to the Senate.

Such is the career of a genuine soldier, who rose to the highest grade in the army. Long after veterans of our day who tell of the prowess of "Little Phil" have passed away, his fame will live in history, and grow the brighter, too, since the dramatic elements coupled with his most illustrious achievements are such as men in all ages remember and admire.

THE LAST SCENES IN THE LIFE OF THE HEROIC SOLDIER.

THE change in the General's condition occurred suddenly. He was lying partially on one side, and the nurse, one of the Sisters who had been in constant attendance, did not notice anything untoward. It had been the practice of the physicians to fre-

quently apply the fingers to the pulse, and Dr.
O'Reilly usually did so.   To his horror on this occasion he discovered great weakness and frequent
intermissions.   He summoned his assistant, and the
first step taken was to administer ammonia.   This
powerful stimulant was powerless to produce a
change in the heart's action.   Digitalis was then in-
jected hypodermically.   Still the life current cours-
ing through the artery at the wrist remained weak.
Then it grew weaker and weaker.   Sinapism was
applied to the chest and limbs, and finally the gal-
vanic battery was brought out, and a current stead-
ily increasing in strength was directed along the
spine and through the chest of the now nearly unconscious form of the pride and joy of the army.

There were no convulsions, no sighing respira-
tion, no rolling of the eyes, none indeed of the phy-
sical signs which attend the departure of the breath
from the human body in many cases of death.
Until within a few minutes of the end Mrs. Sheridan was not greatly alarmed, and she expected a
reaction from the syncope.   Quietly, like a child
going to slumber, the gallant soldier fell into the
last long sleep.   The great heart ceased to beat, and
General Phil Sheridan was dead.

The scene at the bedside was impressive, but was
free from any striking incidents.   During the first
part of the attack General Sheridan did not realize
his condition.   It would appear as if he became
aware of the impending doom before his wife appreciated the danger.   He spoke of his children once
in faint tones, and his manner impressed Mrs. Sheridan for the first time with the fact that her hus-

band was dying. Several family matters were referred to, and he spoke the name of his son. " Little
Phil !" the dying hero whispered, "Little Phil !"

Drs. O'Reilly and Mathews formally requested a
post-mortem examination, being desirous of ascertaining the exact pathological conditions ; but Mrs.
Sheridan, after deliberation, declined to accede to
the request, as there was no reasonable doubt as to
the cause of death, and she did not wish the body
of her husband mutilated.

One of the physicians stated that the valves of
the aorta and of the pulmonary artery were degen-
erated, and that there were atheromatous changes
of the valves of the endocardial lining of the heart.
The impaired circulation of the blood resulting from
these lesions led to the pulmonary engorgement and
the cough of the past.   The heart slowly but defi-
nitely ceased to act.   There had been no indications
of liver, kidney, or other disease.   There was no
dropsical swelling of the legs, and the mind had
only suffered from sympathy with the bodily weakness.   There had been extreme muscular prostra-
tion, and this condition had changed for the better
slowly.   The diet had been restricted because of the
tendency of the stomach to reject much food.
General Sheridan's appetite had not been strong,
and he had had food much as he desired, except on
certain exceptional occasions when his wishes had
to be restrained.

General Sheridan always expressed an aversion to
display in a funeral.   Of course he did not object to
a military demonstration, but nothing resembling a
pageant accorded with his tastes.

AT THE FUNERAL.

THE funeral day of Sheridan, August 11, was warm, clear, cloudless. St. Matthew's is a little, irregular, somewhat old-fashioned church in the official part of Washington. A sultry haze seemed to enfold it. Long before the doors opened a courteous, patient company surrounded them. The little church, oblong, almost square, was decked with the military and mourning emblems.

Crape fluttered from sacred images. Masses of flowers in various forms were piled up under the Virgin's altar—the shoulder-strap of a general in blue and yellow flowers, an easel with vines, a white cross from the President, palms, clustered bunches of pond-lilies, and a wreath. Before the high altar was a raised platform, draped in black, fringed with white. On this rested a coffin, which seemed very small, covered with black cloth, the handles gilded, draped by an American flag, almost covering it—folded and carelessly trailing over the sides. There was a silken sash, emblem of the General's command. At the head was a draped headquarters flag, such as was carried in war. Around it were tall candles and candelabra in which small candles were burning. On this coffin lay a sword—the glorious sword of Sheridan.

Famous people, statesmen, soldiers, sailors, illustrious men with names of world-wide celebrity, were escorted to the pews by the martial ushers.

A voluntary, which came from the organ like a wail, and all eyes turned toward a small company,

slowly led up the central isle. Colonel Michael
Sheridan, with the widow of the General leaning on
his arm ; John Sheridan, another brother, with a
striking resemblance to the deceased, portly, spec-
tacled : General Rucker, and two or three members
of the family, all in deep mourning. In front of
the coffin were three velveted chairs and *pries-dieu.*
In the center, Mrs. Sheridan, with a brother on each
side, knelt in prayer.

Priests, acolytes, groups of boys, with purple and
scarlet trimmings above their white gowns, clustered around the altar. The church began its
sacred offices of repose and intercession. The tall
candles around the bier were lighted, and burned
freely in the gentle breeze which escaped from the
sultry, drowsy sun. The chancel swarmed with
clergymen in various stages of authority, and all
knelt as, following an uplifted cross, the spare form
of the Cardinal, robed in scarlet, wearing the
beretta, slowly moved from the sacristy, knelt at
the altar, and was escorted to the episcopal
throne.

As His Eminence bent in prayer there was a
rustle of interest, as another group moved up the
aisle under military escort—the President, Mrs.
Cleveland, and Mrs. Folsom. And in presence of
an audience representing the statesmanship, the
valor, the history, learning and prosperity of the
nation, the Church began its solemn and beautiful
service for the dead.

The mass was beautifully sung. It was Schmidt's
mass, one of the simplest in musical composition.

CARDINAL GIBBONS'S SERMON.

The following is the text of Cardinal Gibbons's sermon:

"And Jonathan and Simon took Judas their brother, and buried him in the sepulcher of their fathers, in the city of Modin. And all the people of Israel bewailed him with great lamentation ; and they mourned for him many days, and said: How is the mighty fallen that saved the people of Israel?"—I. Mach. ix., 19-21.

Well might the children of Israel bewail their great captain, who led them so often to battle and to victory. And well may this nation grieve for the loss of the mighty chieftain whose mortal remains now lie before us. In every city and town and village of this country, from the Atlantic to the Pacific, his name is uttered with sorrow and his great deeds recorded with admiration.

There is one consoling feature that distinguishes the obsequies of our illustrious hero from those of the great Hebrew leader. He was buried in the midst of war, amid the clashing of arms and surrounded by the armed hosts of the enemy. Our captain, thank God, is buried amid profound peace, while we are enjoying the blessings of domestic tranquillity and are in friendship with all the world.

The death of General Sheridan will be lamented not only by the North, but also by the South. I know the Southern people ; I know their chivalry, I know their magnanimity, their warm and affec-

tionate nature ; and I am sure that the sons of the
South, and especially those who fought in the late
war, will join in the national lamentation and will
lay a garland of mourning on the bier of the great
general. They recognize the fact that the nation's
general is dead, and that his death is the nation's
loss.

And this universal sympathy, coming from all
sections of the country, irrespective of party lines,
is easily accounted for when we consider that under
an overruling Providence the war in which General
Sheridan took such a conspicuous part has resulted
in increased blessings to every State of our common
country.

> " There's a divinity that shapes our ends,
> Rough-hew them how we will."

And this is true of nations as well as of individ.
uals.

What constitutes the great difference between
the wars of antiquity and our recent war ? The war
of the olden time was followed by subjugation and
bondage ; in the train of our great struggle came
reconciliation and freedom. Alexander the Great
waded through the blood of his fellow-man. By the
sword he conquered, and by the sword he kept the
vanquished in bondage. Scarcely was he cold in
death when his vassals shook off the yoke and his
empire was dismembered into fragments.

The effect of the late war has been to weld together the nation still more closely into one cohe-
sive body. It has removed once for all slavery, the
great apple of discord ; it has broken down the wall
of separation which divided section from section,

A BIVOUAC FEAST.

and exhibits us more strikingly as one nation, one family, with the same aims and the same aspirations. The humanity exhibited in our late struggle contrasted with the cruelties exercised toward the vanquished of former times is an eloquent tribute to the blessings of Christian civilization.

In surveying the life of General Sheridan it seems to me that these were his prominent features and the salient points in his character: Undaunted heroism, combined with gentleness of disposition; strong as a lion in war, gentle as a child in peace; bold, daring, fearless, undaunted, unhesitating, his courage rising with the danger; ever fertile in resources, ever prompt in execution, his rapid movements never impelled by blind impulse, but ever prompted by a calculating mind.

I have neither the time nor the ability to dwell upon his military career from the time he left West Point till the close of the war. Let me select one incident which reveals to us his quickness of conception and readiness of execution. I refer to his famous ride in the valley of Virginia. As he is advancing along the road he sees his routed army rushing pell-mell toward him. Quick as thought— by the glance of his eye, by the power of his word, by the strength of his will—he hurls back that living stream on the enemy and snatches victory from the jaws of defeat. How bold in war, how gentle in peace!

On some few occasions in Washington I had the pleasure of meeting General Sheridan socially in private circles. I was forcibly struck by his gentle disposition, his amiable manner, his unassuming deportment, his eye beaming with good-nature, and his voice scarcely raised above a whisper. I said to myself, "Is this bashful man and retiring citizen the great general of the American army? Is this the hero of so many battles?"

It is true General Sheridan has been charged with being sometimes unnecessarily severe toward the enemy. My conversations with him strongly impressed me with the groundlessness of a charge which could in no wise be reconciled with the abhorrence which he expressed for the atrocities of war, with his natural aversion to bloodshed, and with the hope he uttered that he would never again be obliged to draw his sword against an enemy. I am persuaded that the sentiments of humanity ever found a congenial home, a secure lodgment in the breast of General Sheridan. Those who are best acquainted with his military career unite in saying that he never needlessly sacrificed human life, and that he loved and cared for his soldiers as a father loves and cares for his children.

But we must not forget that if the departed hero was a soldier he was too a citizen, and if we wish to know how a man stands as a citizen we must ask ourselves how he stands as a son, a husband, and a father. The parent is the source of the family, the family is the source of the nation. Social life is the reflex of the family life. The stream does not rise above its source. Those who were admitted into the inner circle of General Sheridan's home need not be told that it was a peaceful and happy one. He was a fond husband and an affectionate father, lovingly devoted to his wife and children. I hope I am not trespassing upon the sacred privacy of domestic life when I state that the General's sickness was accelerated, if not aggravated, by a fatiguing journey which he made in order to be home in time to assist at a domestic celebration in which one of his children was the central figure.

Above all, General Sheridan was a Christian. He died fortified by the consolations of religion, having his trust in the saving mercies of our Redeemer and a humble hope of a blessed immortality.

What is life without the hope of immortality? What is life that is bounded by the horizon of the tomb? Sure, it is not worth living. What is the life even of the antediluvian patriarchs but like the mist which is dispelled by the morning sun? What would it profit this illustrious hero to go down to his honored grave covered with earthly glory if he had no hope in the eternal glory to come? It is the hope of eternal life that constitutes at once our dignity and our moral responsibility.

God has planted in the human breast an irresistible desire for immortality. It is born with us and lives and moves with us. It inspires our best and holiest actions. Now, God would not have given us this desire if He did not intend that it should be fully satisfied. He would not have given us this thirst for infinite happiness if He had not intended to assuage it. He never created anything in vain.

Thanks to God, this universal yearning of the human heart is sanctioned and vindicated by the voice of revelation.

The inspired Word of God not only proclaims the

immortality of the soul but also the future resurrection of the body. "I know," says the prophet Job, "that my Redeemer liveth, and that on the last day I shall rise out of the earth and in my flesh I shall see my God." "Wonder not at this," says our Saviour, "for the hour cometh when all that are in their graves shall hear the voice of the Son of Man, and they who have done well shall come forth to the resurrection of life, and they that have done ill to the resurrection of judgment." And the Apostle writes in these comforting words to the Thessalonians: "I would not have you ignorant, brethren, concerning those that are asleep, that ye be not sorrowful like those who have no hope; for if we believe that Jesus died and rose again, even so those who have died in Jesus, God will raise unto himself. Therefore comfort yourself with these words."

These are the words of comfort I would address to you, madam, faithful consort of the illustrious dead. This is the olive-branch of peace and hope I would bring you to-day. This is the silver lining of the cloud which hangs over you. We followed you in spirit and with sympathizing hearts as you knelt in prayer at the bed of your dying husband. May the God of all consolation comfort you in this hour of sorrow. May the soul of your husband be this day in peace and his abode in Zion; may his memory be ever enshrined in the hearts of his countrymen, and may our beloved country, which he has loved and served so well, ever be among the foremost nations of the earth, the favored land of constitutional freedom, strong in the loyalty of its

patriotic citizens and in the genius and valor of its
soldiers till time shall be no more.

Comrades and companions of the illustrious dead,
take hence your great leader, bear him to his last
resting-place, carry him gently, lovingly ; and
though you may not hope to attain his exalted rank
you will strive at least to emulate him by the in-
tegrity of your private life, by your devotion to
your country, and by upholding the honor of your
military profession.

The sermon ended, the Cardinal, assuming the
elaborate robes of his office, coped and mitred, the
cross borne before him and priests holding his
train, took his place at the foot of the coffin and
read the prayers of the Church in Latin and then in
English.

And while the sweet, entreating voice of the Cardinal voiced these tender offices of the dead, and
from the trained company of priests and musicians
came the answering entreaty that God would be
with the dead and have mercy for evermore, through
the windows came a quick, instant sound of command, the bugle note, the tramp of armed men
moving into column, the crash of the muskets as
they came heavily to the ground. It was a strange
unison—peace and war, repose and action. The
Church and the State seemed to blend and to com-
bine to do honor to the memory of the dead.

The offices of the Church and the weird, mournful
chants rose and fell as the martial notes of preparation fell strangely, but not harshly, on the ear.
For it was fitting that the bugle notes should be

heard in such a ceremony. The last word before the altar had been spoken, and at a signal a body of grizzled, brown soldiers and officers marched up the aisle with firm military stride to the coffin. The pall bearers formed in line, Sherman and Carlisle leading.

The grave of Sheridan is on a slope almost immediately in front of the Arlington mansion, not a hundred paces from the door. Here on the brow of the hill, where you have one of the most beautiful views imaginable, even in picturesque Virginia, Sheridan finds rest. It seems fitting that the spirit of Sheridan should stand forever, as it were, keeping watch and ward over the Capitol he defended and saved.

The artillery were massed at the foot of the hill, the guns ready to fire. The infantry drew up in line, extending down the slope. The grave had been covered with rude scantling, which was torn away as the procession advanced.

Tenderly the coffin was laid in its place. The flag was lovingly removed. The glorious sword of the dead hero, which seemed rusted and worn with service, was reverently taken from the coffin by an aid. Then the company were pressed back while the batteries saluted and the infantry fired three volleys. A bugler, one who had served under Sheridan, came to the grave and played the old bugle notes of "taps." It was the good-night he had heard as a boy at the military school, as an officer during his whole army life—meaning that the day was ended and that the work was done. As at the grave of Grant, so at the grave of Sheridan, was the same felicitous thought—that the ceremony should end with the old bugle notes.

In accordance with the wishes of Mrs. Sheridan the funeral was a strictly military affair, and the escort was formed precisely as prescribed by the army regulations for an officer of the rank of the deceased.

HIS LIFE AT WASHINGTON.

GEN. SHERIDAN was not married until nine years after the war, but then began a domestic life whose uninterrupted happiness beautifully rounded his career. He was in the prime of life when he met Miss Irene Rucker, the daughter of Gen. Rucker, who became his wife. Gen. Sheridan first met her at a marriage in army circles, at which she was a bridesmaids, and at once succumbed to her charms. Only those who have been intimate in that domestic circle can tell of its harmony. The young wife, almost twenty years her famous husband's junior, had all the pride in his career that the daughter of an army officer, reared to appreciate the triumphs of war, alone could know.

She came from a family of soldiers, and her father, grandfather and two brothers were all officers of high rank in the service. Her father, Major-Gen. Daniel Henry Rucker, a native of Belleville, N. J., entered the army from Michigan as lieutenant of dragoons in 1837, and served distinction on the frontiers, in the Cherokee Nation, at Fort Leavenworth, and in Texas and Mexico. From 1853 to

1855 he was stationed at Fort Union as depot quartermaster, and it was at this military post that Mrs. Sheridan was born.

The first three years of Mrs. Sheridan's infant life were passed at that frontier fort amid the alarms of Indian wars and the discomforts of garrison life. The following year was passed at Detroit, where her father was stationed. From that point he was transferred to Washington. There Mrs. Sheridan passed several years of her early childhood.

Upon the outbreak of the war, her father having been assigned to duty in the field, and being surrounded by the turmoils of military concentration and movements at the capital, she was placed with her younger sister Sara, who was born at Albuquerque, another frontier post in New Mexico, at the Georgetown (now West Washington) Academy of the Visitation, and remained there until the close of the war. Her father having been ordered to Philadelphia for duty, Miss Rucker and her sister were placed at the School of the Convent of the Sisters of the Holy Child at that city.

Gen. Sheridan was always a much-sought companion for a festal gathering. His robust health, his happy home relations, his proud military achievements, have all combined to round out to perfection the genial character of the ideal commander.

When he went to Washington after the retirement of Gen. Sherman, his friends in Chicago were desirous of giving him a testimonial of their friendship, and subscribed a sufficient sum of money to

THE GUNBOAT MONTICELLO RESCUING FUGITIVES.

purchase a comfortable and attractive home. The house selected is situated on the northeast corner of Rhode Island Avenue and Seventeenth Street.

The office of Lieutenant-General of the Army died with him, as did the office of General of the Army disappear with the retirement of Gen. Sherman.

In one corner of the large parlor stands a mahogany cabinet filled with curios and relics representing some of the leading facts of the General's life. The meerschaum pipe that he had smoked throughout the war lies here. It is well colored and its steady use is shown by the burning off of the edge of the bowl. Here are beautiful canes, curiously carved, the gift of many a friend ; there are swords of various shapes and sizes, wrought with gold and with silver ; there are canteens, rare coins, beautiful medals and all sorts of souvenirs of the General's adventurous life. Everything has some historical or personal reminiscence connected with it, and the whole atmosphere speaks of a well-deserved comfort. There are stuffed birds and animals, a magnificent Mexican saddle, with bridle and lariat to match, with a sombrero hung beside it. This was the gift of a friend in Mexico, and its trappings are such that it took years to make it.

The deep love of Gen. Sheridan for the animal creation is evidenced by the presence in many of the rooms of stuffed animals, which look down from the walls in greeting to the visitor. In the dining-room there are among the china some rare pieces. A pitcher of white and gold has an excellent picture of Gen. Grant burned in one side and that of Gen. Sheridan on the other. A solid silver dish-tray was given Gen. Sheridan by friends in Chicago. A splendid oil portrait of the General in the parlor represents him in full uniform upon the field of battle.

ANECDOTES AND REMINISCENCES OF THE GREAT SOLDIER,

AS RELATED BY THOSE WHO KNEW HIM AND FOUGHT WITH HIM.

COL. BURR'S REMINISCENCES.

"KEEP the enemy always in sight," was Grant's order to Sheridan, as he started him for the Shenandoah Valley in that doubtful battle summer of 1864. Well did the great cavalryman follow his chief's instructions. Sheridan's wonderful powers were first made manifest to the nation in the campaign which followed his transfer from the "On to Richmond" line to the valley of Virginia. Three years of desperate warfare had been waged, and he had attained the rank of Major-General without the country appreciating his capacity as a commander. It is true he had done some brilliant things. Starting even as late as 1862, as a commissary on Gen. Halleck's staff, he was made a Brigadier-General in one month after he was given an opportunity to show his quality. It has been written that "all the great opportunities of life come to us through an accident." Sheridan's career would seem to prove the truth of this saying. He was appointed Colonel of the Second Michigan Cavalry without his knowledge. Coming from Ohio, he had naturally expected a regiment of volunteers from his own State, but the authorities turned a deaf ear to his appeals, and it remained for Michigan to start the great General on his remarkable career. Only the day after his appointment he took command of the organization of which I had the honor to be a member. None of the veterans of the old Second Michigan will ever forget his first appearance on dress parade. He was anything but the typical hero ; small in stature, with short legs and broad shoulders, he appeared a singular figure to the thousand men who faced him on that May day in 1862 when he for the first time gave an order to the regiment.

Gordon Granger had been our Colonel, and in some respects he was an ideal soldier, but the new commander was so small in stature that the boys at once began discussing his powers with a sort of dubious shake of the head. Two days later he moved with his regiment in Col. Elliott's brigade for a raid upon Booneville. This was the first successful raid of the war on the Union side, and accomplished a great deal in the way of tearing up the Mobile & Ohio Railroad and destroying war supplies at this vantage-point on that line of railway. During this episode every officer and man of the Second Michigan Cavalry was taught a wholesome respect for the fighting quality of the new Colonel, whom they named " Little Phil."

The occupation of Corinth compelled the Union

forces to extreme vigilance, as the enemy was in
force and still held the railroad arteries, of which
the Mobile & Ohio road was the most important.
Gen. Gordon Granger, who had made the Second
Michigan Cavalry as its first Colonel the efficient
organization that Sheridan found it to be, was in
command of Halleck's cavalry division. It consisted of two brigades, of which the second was
formed of the Second Iowa, Col. Elliott, and the
Second Michigan, Col. Sheridan. On the 28th of
May, 1862, this brigade, by a circuitous route, was
sent to strike the railroad at some point thirty or
forty miles below Corinth. After a sharp skirmish
at Booneville, the Confederate cavalry was driven
out and the place captured. A large quantity of
small arms, artillery, ammunition, a large number
of cars, locomotives, etc., besides nearly 3000 sick,
wounded and convalescent soldiers were taken.
The depot was burned, the road cut and destroyed
in several places, and the brigade returned unmolested to Farmington. A sharp fight occurred on
the 4th of June, near Booneville, in which Sheridan
participated with his command. Again on the 6th
he encountered a regiment of Confederate cavalry
and drove it back with loss into a large body of
infantry. Again at other dates up to the last of
June Sheridan was actively engaged.

All this was but the prelude to his first action,
but it serves to show the quality of the man. He
was soon assigned to the command of the Second
Brigade, and on the 28th of June established his
headquarters at Booneville.

On the 1st of July a Confederate cavalry force,

under command of General Chalmers, advanced from the South upon the post. The attack began early in the morning upon a picket of the Second Michigan, under Lieut. Scranton. They fell back slowly to the point of intersection of a second road, where a second company, under Capt. Campbell, was stationed. The fight began in earnest, a natural barricade was found, and, under cover, the advancing enemy was brought to a halt. The contest became stubborn and the fighting superb, but finding the Confederates gaining ground, three more companies were sent to the point, under command of Capt. Campbell, also of the Second Michigan.

Confident now, Chalmers deployed two regiments on the right of the road, thus overlapping the Union front so far that by merely curving the wings inward the whole force would have been surrounded. Sheridan quickly sent word to Capt. Campbell to hold the ground at all hazards until reinforced, but, if pushed beyond endurance to fall back slowly. Col. Hatch, of the Second Iowa, was then sent to support him, with orders to charge wherever he could best strike the enemy. In the open field, meanwhile, the gray-coated horsemen, in well-closed ranks, waited until the skirmishers had driven the Michigan troops well together; then, with shouts, they swept down, each man eager to be first in the capture. Ordered to reserve their fire until the enemy was within twenty-five or thirty yards' range, the Union men obeyed. On came the solid Confederate battalions. A storm of bullets withered the first line and was the reply to an order for surrender. Others followed, for the smallness of the force was, to some extent, made up by their possession of Colt's revolving rifles, which carried five shots without reloading. These men were good marksmen also. So well were the rifles used that the charge was stayed. Again the Confederates closed up their lines and swept back on the flank of the struggling Wolverines. Still fighting inch by inch, the later fell slowly back, keeping at bay the overwhelming enemy. Again Chalmers charged in line with loud yells as of assured victory. The Union men, having no time to reload, used their guns as clubs to ward off their overconfident enemies. It was a desperate moment. But again Sheridan sent in another timely supply of men from his slender line. The combat had lasted from daylight, and it was now afternoon, Chalmers made a wide sweep and came in on the left of the Union camp, almost within gun-shot of the tents. There was no sign of the reinforcements by rail for which Sheridan had asked. Still he had no thought of giving up. But the young soldier's resources were wofully slender for either valor or strategy. Meagre as they were they sufficed him. While 2000 Confederates were besetting the 400 men on the Blackland road, and 2000 more were swinging into line at the very gates of the camp on the east, Sheridan hurried to the tent of Capt. Alger, who was lying sick with camp-fever. He was asked to take charge of a desperate venture, and readily agreed to do his share in the crisis.

Sheridan had parked his wagon train on the low ground to the west and north of the town, and prepared for a last desperate stand. Besides this, he had hurried two companies in line, one from the Second Michigan and one from the Second Iowa. There were ninety-two men in all in this little band, which he intrusted to Capt. Alger. To better inspire them with the spirit of rivalry, he had taken one company from each regiment in his command instead of taking both companies from the same regiment. When Alger was mounted, Sheridan directed him to move off to the right and strike the enemy in the rear. He spoke privately of the desperate risks to be taken, and indicated the exact moment at which he should strike the foe. Alger was to leave Booneville by a wood road running westward, moving until he reached a point in a covered lane where an old negro would be found to guide him to the point of attack. Sheridan's instructions were so minute, and he showed such perfect familiarity with the country, that he inspired confidence in the officer to whom he had intrusted this dangerous errand.

This early incident aptly illustrated his power as a soldier and commander. Short as had been Sheridan's stay in Booneville, he knew more of the country than the rebels themselves. He always made it his first duty to memorize every foot of the territory that he might be called upon to defend or contest. Napoloen and all great or capable commanders have had this faculty. Sheridan had not been twenty-four hours at Booneville before he had mapped in his mind every road, lane, farm, hill, or natural impediment that might play an important part in action. It was to a visit to the neighborhood of

Waterloo, long before he confronted Napoleon, that Wellington owed his escape from the French after his defeat at Quatre Bras. Given equal numbers in combat, the man who knows the topography best is almost certain to win the battle. Sheridan knew his map by heart. He knew the character of the people and the nature of all surroundings. The attack he was now called upon to resist found him equipped with everything except men that the craft and energy of a leader could command. He had also a trusty scout who lived in the neighborhood— a light complexioned, long-haired Mississippian, with a keen eye and cadaverous form. Reticent and modest, this partisan had the confidence of both officers and men. To him was intrusted the conduct of the "forlorn hope" to the negro's rendezvous. Nothing was left to chance. Capt. Alger knew that the salvation of the whole command depended upon his courage, activity and vigor. Perhaps it was just as well that the men did not appreciaee the madness of their undertaking. It takes more than ordinary courage for ninety-two men to assault 4000, especially when, as in this case, every chance was against them. They were to traverse an unknown country by divers roads, through deep woods, and were to meet at the end of the march an overwhelming enemy, in the midst of a treacherous population. As the men moved off Sheridan said to Capt. Alger:

"Don't dismount your men in any event! Don't deploy them, or you will show the enemy the weakness of your force. Charge in column, and, if possible, come through and join me. When you make

SHERIDAN IN THE SHENANDOAH VALLEY (OCTOBER, 1864)—THE DEFEAT OF GENERAL ROSSER, AND STRUGGLE FOR THE LAST CONFEDERATE GUN AT MOUNT JACKSON.

the assault, shout and make all the noise possible !
When I hear you I will strike them in front. I
have carefully gauged the time, and whether I
hear from you or not, in one hour I shall charge
them."

In all these directions the quality of the man as
a commander is clearly seen. They outline his
ready brain as a silhouette does the lines of face and
head. Every instruction was obeyed, and the forlorn hope reached the rear of the enemy. "Forward, men!" Capt. Alger commands.

It was an audacious move. In a scant column of
fours the daring troopers trotted on up the Blackland road to a point where no attack was expected.
Chalmers's headquarters were reached and captured.
Capt. Schuyler, of the Second Iowa, was left to look
after those captured there and to watch the left of
the road. Alger dashed on. Sheridan was watch-
ing, strained and anxious. The onset was not heard.
It was too far for the voices of such a handful to
span with sound.

When the hand pointed to the last moment of the
hour, Sheridan prepared for the charge. Just as
he moved out a train came down the road and drew
into Booneville, sounding its shrill whistle as a warning and a welcome to those who were in the battle.
Every one in the Union lines knew that Sheridan
had sent for reinforcements, and the arrival of the
train filled the struggling soldiers with a new hope.
They began to cheer, and the train-men joined with
a will. Sheridan made prompt use of the timely
incident. He sent word to the engineer to keep up
whistling, and to the train hands to cheer and make

such clatter as would imply fresh men. The civil-
ians took the hint. There was a pandemonium of
yells and huzzas. At this moment Sheridan swung
his tired battalions into line. The men caught the
inspiration of their commander and felt with him
the responsibilities of the moment. Half a mile in
front of them were the gray masses, moving in and
out in busy preparation for the final onset.

The scene on both sides was a spirited one, but
there was no time for reflection. Sheridan is in
front. He shouts to his troops, "Forward!" The
squadrons sweep across the fields in close order.
As they draw near, dropping shots from the Confederate artillery and carbines empty a saddle here
and there. Still on they go. No one has thought
for anything but the enemy. The excitement of
the charge thrills every nerve. The lust of battle
shines in every eye. They draw closer and closer
to the foe. Each bluecoat singles out his man, and
with a crash as of meeting waters, and a yell as of
contending demons, the two forces come together.
The Confederate line wavers and then breaks before
the force of that charge. At this moment Alger's
handful, like a missile loosed from a catapult, was
flung upon the enemy. This unexpected attack
threw them into great confusion. The uproar of
Sheridan's charge drowned the shouts of Alger's
men. Their danger became great. The "forlorn
hope" had achieved its task, but now itself was in
a desperate scramble with flying Confederates. Beyond the reach of aid from Sheridan, it was in a
running fight with the enemy, who, as they broke
to the rear, tried to punish the Alger force for its

temerity. In the melee each side sought to do all the damage it could to the other, while getting out of danger itself. Our little command were rushing to the rear with as much speed as their enemy. They had emptied their revolvers into a confused mass of Confederates, which they had driven off by the roadside. Ammunition was gone, and they plied the sabre unsparingly.

The Confederates were in point of numbers vastly superior. But they pushed off the field fighting as they ran. Alger himself rode side by side with a Confederate, each emptying his revolver without doing any injury. As Alger had finished his last shot he was carried, partly by the antics of his horse and partly by the rush of those about him, beyond his own men and into the timber, where the enemy were also seeking shelter. His unmanageable horse ran until a limb tore the luckless rider from his saddle, breaking his ribs as he swung violently against the tree. He had barely strength to parry a vicious blow from a flying cavalryman as he fell into the thick underbrush, unconscious. How long he lay he never knew. When he recovered consciousness all was quiet about him. The Confederates had disappeared and so had his command. He dragged himself from his shelter, crawled to the road, and had entered an open field when the clatter of horses' hoofs reached his ears. He thought it might be the enemy and concealed himself. But they were from the Second Iowa. Sherman had sent them out to seek him, though it was thought that he had been killed. They put him on a horse and returned to camp. It was after dark when

Sheridan greeted him with "Old fellow, you have done well." Capt. Alger lost more than half of his command, and the Confederates were many more men short from the effects of Sheridan's first charge. For this day's work Sheridan was made a brigadier, and Alger gained a majority. The commander had never received his commission nor been mustered in as Colonel. Gov. Blair had "appointed" him, and accidentally delayed the forwarding of his commission on his own return to Lansing, Mich.

The campaign won for Sheridan full recognition and the respect also of the enemy. Gen. Rosecrans, in a general order, said:

"The coolness, determination, and fearless gallantry displayed by Col. Sheridan and the officers and men of his command deserve the thanks and admiration of the army."

Sheridan had 728 men; Chalmers, 4700; the fighting lasted eight hours; our losses numbered 41 killed, wounded, and missing, and the enemy, carrying off its wounded, left 65 dead on the field. Gen. Halleck from Corinth asked for Sheridan's promotion.

The fight in itself was comparatively a small affair; in its conduct and results it was of magnifying importance. It created a commander, it gave him his first chance, it taught the men in command and the country at large that a new force had arrived. It showed every quality of command. Skilful handling of troops, nerve and audacity to the outmost, that superb mental map-making which a successful soldier must possess, which Grant with

Sherman and Thomas had, McClellan missed in part, and Halleck never possessed ; and it also gave evidence on a small scale of that same strategetical power which Five Forks exhibited on such a larger one.

The battle of Booneville made him a Brigadier-General, but no great opportunity arose for him to show his mettle. After his promotion he was assigned to an infantry command, and his appearance again in battle was on October 8, 1862, at Perryville, Ky. Jackson, whom he had fought with as a cadet at West Point and been suspended for a time, had been killed. Rosseau was in trouble when Sheridan moved his division up, struck the enemy hard and saved the day. He then moved with the army to Nashville and became a significant division commander in the reorganized Army of the Cumberland under Rosecrans. Stone River was his next battle, at the close of the year, Dec. 31. Here his work was so well done that he received the warm commendations of his superiors. The Tullahoma campaign, from July to September, 1863, then followed, to end at Chickamauga. Here Sheridan had his second wrestle with Cheatham and won the applause of the defeated army for his brilliant share in the engagement where he reformed his division after the rout and returned to the field. Missionary Ridge in 1864, and the two days of picturesque battles which preceded it, found Sheridan, with Grant, Sherman, Thomas and Hooker, a central figure of that wonderful series of battles which ended in the defeat of Bragg's army.

Grant's fame was now at its full tide. He was

called East and made Lieutenant-General.   He wanted a cavalryman.   His mind instinctively sought out Sheridan, the greatest trooper in the world's history.   When he crossed the Rapidan, in April, 1864, as commander of all of the cavalry of the Army of the Potomac, he had his first real opportunity to show how well he knew the arts and chances of war.   He covered the flank's advance and communications through all the terrible days of May, June and July.   His bold swing to the rear of the Confederate army after the Wilderness and march for Richmond was a great movement both in conception and accomplishment.   He reached within seven miles of Richmond without a serious battle, save Yellow Tavern, where J. E. B. Stuart, the great Southern rough-rider, was killed by the Fifth Michigan cavalry.   Early's advance on Washington, August, 1864, sent Sheridan to the Shenandoah Valley.   At first he only commanded the cavalry, but finally he was given all the forces, and in 1864, for the first time in his career, he became commander of an army and a central and picturesque figure of war.   His wonderful fight with Early at Winchester, where by personal daring he snatched victory from the jaws of defeat, is easily recalled. Then followed Cedar Creek and Fisher's Hill, and a broken and shattered Confederate army attested the force of his blows and the fulness of his prowess as a commander of men on the field.   A grateful nation passed its resolution of thanks, and he stood out in the front rank among the great soldiers of the world.   The early days of spring found him back with Grant.   The great valley he had left a barren plain, without a hostile force of importance in it. After Meade crashed through Lee's lines at Petersburg, Sheridan become the remorseless demon of pursuit to the retreating Confederates.

The battle of Five Forks was perhaps the most ingeniously conceived and most skilfully executed engagement that was ever fought on this continent. It matched in secretiveness and shrewdness the cleverest efforts of Napoleon, and showed also much of that soldier's broadness of intellect and capacity for great occasions.

It was the one opportunity that was necessary to give Sheridan full scope for his genius as a commander of men in the field. Well did he make use of it, and his matchless tactics and splendid bearing at Five Forks made clear his title to the Lieutenant-Generalship which came only a few years since. The world has given its estimate of this battle and the pursuit of Lee, but Grant speaks of it in detail thus :

" It took the humble Ohio lad more than four years, in the white heat of war, to make these facts clear to his countrymen and the authorities in control of the Government and its armies. He was not a typical hero in appearance. His size was against him. Restless, full of the combative quality, not politic in language, somewhat reticent, half stubborn and fond of hazardous enterprises, he was the embodiment of heroism, dash and impulse. Then he had the power of inspiring all about him, and imparting to others the very confidence he felt himself. Yet he seemingly commanded only those qualities which show the wide difference between

the habitual impulses of the brilliant corps commander and the cool thinking of a chief in the art,
as well as in the onset, of war."

At the very outset of his career, just after he was
appointed colonel of cavalry, and while on the
way with his regiment to join Gen. Gordon Granger,
he met the future commander of the armies. But
the impression he created on that occasion was not
a favorable one. In fact, Grant tells us that it was
bad, and relates the incident in these words:

"Sheridan's pursuit of Lee was perfect in its
generalship and energy." Gen. Grant paid this
fitting tribute to the soldier whose brilliant career
is here recorded. "As a soldier, as a commander
of troops, as a man capable of doing all that is possible with any number of men, there is no man living
greater than Sheridan. He belongs to the very
first rank of soldiers, not only of our country, but
of the world. I rank Sheridan with Napoleon and
Frederick and the great commanders in history.
No man ever had such a faculty of finding out
things as Sheridan, or of knowing all about the enemy. Then he had that magnetic quality of sway-
ing men which I wish I had—a rare quality in a
general. I don't think any one can give Sheridan
too high praise.

"We met at a railway station. I had never seen
Sheridan but once before. He was then commissary
at Halleck's headquarters during the march towards
Corinth. Although he belonged to the Fourth Infantry, my old regiment, I had no acquaintance
with him, for he graduated ten years after I had
left West Point. I knew I had sent a regiment of

THE CONFEDERATE SPY IN CAMP.

cavalry to join Granger, but I had not indicated the
Second Michigan, of which Sheridan had recently
been made the Colonel. I really did not wish that
regiment to leave. As we met for the second time
in our lives, I spoke to him about his going. He
said he would rather go than stay, or some similar
brusque and rough remark that annoyed me. I
don't think he could have said anything that would
have made a worse impression upon me. But I
subsequently watched his career and saw how much
there was in him. When I came East and took
command I looked around for a cavalry commander.
While standing in front of the White House talking to Mr. Lincoln and Gen. Halleck, I said I
wanted the best man I could find for a cavalry commander. ' Then,' said Halleck, ' why not take Phil
Sheridan ? ' ' Well,' I said, ' I was going to say
Phil Sheridan.' So Sheridan was sent for and he
came, but very much disgusted. He was just about
to have a corps, and he did not know why we
wanted him East, whether it was to discipline him
or not."

The country had not yet become interested in
Sheridan, as Grant had. He was still practically
unknown outside the immediate army in which he
served when called from the West. His great fight
with Cheatham at Stone River, his second struggle
with the same general at Chickamauga, and his
good deeds at Missionary Ridge had, it is true, attracted the attention of military men. But he was
only at the threshold of his fame when Grant sent
him across the Rapidan as his chief of cavalry in
1864. The troopers had now become a positive

power in army operations, yet their new leader was only considered a "rough rider" by the country— capable of great things with a small force and rapid movement. The series of brilliant cavalry operations which led to his transfer to the Shenandoah was all lost to the public ear in the din of the greater army movements that were going on around him. He was sent to the Valley of Virginia by an accident, as a cavalryman, not as a great commander, but his deeds soon carried him to supreme command, and he fought several great battles. Yet he did not reach the summit of his fame until the final act which destroyed Lee's army. In the closing hours of the Rebellion Sheridan became the vivid omen of defeat to the broken soldier in gray. Grant called him from the Shenandoah, and when he reached him on the last days of February, 1865, with his 10,000 troopers, the lines were closing around the fated Confederacy. Sheridan became to Grant what Murat was to Napoleon. After Meade's forces crashed through Lee's lines at Petersburg and the Southern commander moved south to join Johnston, Sheridan's great work began.

The falling army against which his firm and fateful operations were now directed was simply a vitalized desperation. It was at the mercy of time. It had hopes, but they were only a pathetic disbelief in the inevitable. The swift stroke of the Federal cavalry was everywhere. It flashed upon the Confederate flanks, laughed past its front, and then it picked up the stragglers. It was the materialized sneer of Fate at the hopelessness of further opposition.

The lines were closing, and there were gaps through which the hoof-beats of the horses were heard and the sabres of the troopers fell. Every time they advanced farther and more recklessly, until the doomed army knew that the great cordon which was to crush it was closing more and more tightly around it. The daring of the Confederates was simply an attempt to postpone the inevitable; but it was a striking illustration of their discipline and the confidence reposed in their commander. The cavalry had whirled through the Shenandoah —a cyclone of war—and had left a ruined country and a scattered and dispirited remnant of an army. It had throttled the last hope at Five Forks. Sheridan, the dashing cavalry officer, the masterly leader of men in battle, here proved himself a perfect tactician on the field and in the face of a ⁀ghting army. The whole of his movements won ᵣm an applauding world the recognition of his powers as a great commanding general. From that point it was little more than a series of running skirmishes, some of them desperate, all of them evidences of American grit; for, though sore, weary, and starving, the remnants of Lee's once great army would sometimes turn and sting with terrible power their relentless pursuers. But Union troopers harassed them at every turn. The infantry drove their already dejected forces into disorder. The great cordon closed around them like an immense barn-door, and the main army swung on the veterans of Lee. Like a host of beating flails winnowing the grain, every avenue was closed by the Federal troopers. They had overrun all the roads

of supplies and left them barren. Wherever the
Confederacy looked expectantly for some new path
of escape or succor, Sheridan was there like a
whirlwind of death and defeat. Across fields, down
highways, through by-paths and on every road, in
the storm and terror of Five Forks, on the road
below Appomattox, this great cavalryman and
wonderful soldier was leading the advance or striking the flank of the enemy with an energy born of
the mighty power of a great brain well schooled in
the best element of the art and vigor of war.

Finally, on a beautiful April morning in 1869, as
the sun rose over the hills and vales of a region that
had never yet felt the cruel footfall of war, Sheridan's cavalry swung into line for the last charge.
The sound of those horses' hoofs on the road beyond Gordon's advance was the final menace to the
expiring Confederacy.

The night of the 8th of April closed upon a day
of hard work and exciting events. By a forced and
rapid march Sheridan had thrust his cavalry in front
of the retreating Confederate army. The night before the surrender Custer had enveloped Appomattox
station, capturing three heavily laden railway trains
of supplies, twenty-five pieces of artillery, two hundred wagons, and many prisoners. After this stroke
the cavalrymen stood to horse all night. The gray
of the morning was just yielding to the stronger
light of full day when they were ordered to move
forward. As they emerged from the woods and
advanced upon the plains beyond they could see
the army of Lee cut off from further retreat. It
was a sight at once grand and thrilling when the

horsemen moved forward to the final attack. Gordon made a final attempt to destroy the line of cavalry which appeared with sabres glistening in the spring sun, the trophies of war mingling with battle-flags of the Union commander. Behind Sheridan's cavalry long lines of infantry under Ord, Griffin, and Gibbon were waiting to gather the sheaves of war which Sheridan's troopers had secured. The last fight was a short one, and the white flag of truce from Gordon's headquarters announced the final surrender. Sheridan rode into the Confederate lines to receive the praises of his chief and the applause of his country for his brilliant work. It was a fitting end to the closing hours of the great struggle, that his fame as a soldier should be completed only with the final breaking up, which his generalship and energy had done so much to hasten.

Gen. Sheridan's part in the surrender of Lee was very significant. He was not in good humor on that April morning and was disposed to doubt the sincerity of the Confederate commanders. He fumed and fretted when his charge was stayed by the flag of truce.

GOV. GORDON'S REMINISCENCES.

Gen. Gordon, now Governor of Georgia, tells this story of Sheridan at Appomattox:

A cavalry officer came to me from Sheridan with a flag of truce. He was a handsome fellow and very polite. Saluting, he said :

" 'Is this Gen. Gordon? I am the bearer of Gen.

Sheridan's compliments, and he demands your un-conditional surrender.'

"'Well, Colonel' (or whatever I saw his rank was), I answered, 'you will please return my com-pliments to Gen. Sheridan and say that I shall not surrender.'

"'Then,' he said, 'you will be annihilated in half an hour. We have you completely sur-rounded.'

"'Very well, sir,' I replied, 'I am probably as well aware of my situation as you are, but that is my answer.'

"'You don't mean that!' he exclaimed.

"'Yes, I do, sir,' I said, 'the only thing I pro-pose to say is what I have already said through my staff officer—that a flag of truce is in existence be-tween Gen. Lee and Gen. Grant. I was not going to surrender, because I knew it was coming. I was not going to let Sheridan capture me in that way.''

"'Then you will be annihilated,' he said, and rode away.

"While I had been sitting there, waiting, the firing had almost ceased. The infantry on my flanks had not changed their position much, as they had been moving up very slowly. I was firing artillery at the time, so as to check them. In a few minutes Sheridan himself came up with his staff. He was riding an immense black horse. I will never forget how he looked with his short legs sticking out on either side. We had very much the same sort of parley as had occurred between the other officer and myself. Indeed the language was almost a literal repetition. Finally I said to him : 'General, I hardly think that it is worth while for us to parley. I have made up my mind not to surrender, and I shall accept any consequences that may follow this determination. I wish simply to give you the information which was sent me by Gen. Lee. All I know is that there is a flag of truce in existence, and I only know the bare fact.'

" ' Did you say that you have a letter from Gen. Lee ? ' he asked.

" I handed him the letter.

" He looked it over and said : ' I suppose, then, that the only thing we can do is to cease firing.'

" ' I think so,' I replied.

" He then said to me : ' If you will withdraw your forces to a certain place, I will withdraw mine, and wint to see what happens.'

" We got down off our horses, and taking a seat on the grass talked there for some time. In the mean time I had forgotten that early in the morning I had detached a force to go back and over on the brow of a hill to prevent the cavalry from coming around between Longstreet and myself. While we were sitting on the grass I heard a roll of musketry, and looking over to where the force had been placed saw it firing into some cavalry that had ridden down in that direction.

" ' Sir, what does this mean ? ' cried Sheridan.

" ' I am very sorry about it,' I replied, as I explained the circumstances, and he and I each sent an officer over to the hill to stop the firing.

" I saved Sheridan's life that morning beyond

question.   One of my sharpshooters was a sour sort
of fellow, and his only idea was that when he saw
a blue coat it was his duty to shoot at it.   I had
the sharpshooters around me when Sheridan came
up with the flag of truce, and I saw this fellow draw
his gun.   'What do you mean?' I cried, 'this is a
flag of truce.'   He did not pay the slightest attention to me, and was just about firing when I knocked
up his gun and it went off, over Sheridan's head.
'Let him stay on his own side, General,' he mut-
tered.

    "Gen. Sheridan and I sat on the ground, close to
the brick house where Lee and Grant met, in the
orchard.   I had passed the house in the morning.
We chaffed each other a little in the course of the
conversation, Sheridan saying: 'I believe I had
the pleasure of meeting you before.'   I replied that
we had had some little acquaintance in the Valley
of Virginia.   He turned the thread of the conversation to some guns he had received in the valley.
Sheridan had captured nearly all of Early's artillery and some more had been sent to him from
Richmond.   Some wag had written with chalk on
one of those guns: 'Respectfully consigned to
Major-Gen. Sheridan through Early.'   Sheridan
had heard of this, and he was very much amused
at it; but whether he ever saw such words upon a
gun I do not know.   When he was through with
his story I suggested that I also had two guns
which I could consign to him, and with the more
grace because they had come from him that very
morning.

    "Sheridan came with a full staff and remained

U. S. Grant.

with me about an hour and a half. My recollection
is that we stayed at that place until we received
information that Gen. Lee and Gen. Grant had
agreed.''

INCIDENTS IN HIS LIFE.

ONE of the most interesting periods of Gen.
Sheridan's life is that of his early boyhood. A
gentleman who played a very important part in the
early life of the General relates the following
story. He knew Sheridan as a boy, and his contri-
bution to the soldier's life is interesting :

'' Phil Sheridan was born at Somerset, O., and
he spent his boyhood there. His father was a
teamster, and brought goods from Zanesville and
Lancaster to the little merchants of Somerset. I
can remember him very well as a toddler, and when
he got a little older he was employed by a firm
of general merchants named Fink & Ditto. Fink
was a great big, burly fellow, who did all the
rough work, and Ditto was a little, sedate man,
and wore gold spectacles, and they were both old
line Whigs. Phil's duty was to open the store
and sweep out, and he did it well. He had a
brother, Patrick, who was a clerk in the store,
but summer and winter little Phil was at the store
bright and early. He was liked universally and
always spoken of as a most polite little fellow.
Well, the member of Congress from that district
was old Tom Ritchie, a man well known as having
lots of good sense, but little education. I used to

write his letters for him, for he was a farmer and
said he did not have time to write. One day he
came into my office with about fifty letters in his
hand. He threw them down on my desk and said :
'I have opened only one of these, but I know what
they are all about. These people all want their sons
appointed to West Point, and I am about to make
one friend and forty-nine enemies.' I looked at
him for a moment and said I would tell him how he
could avoid making any enemies. When he asked
how, I said : 'Send Phil Sheridan to West Point.'
The idea seemed to strike the old man in the right
spot, and he gave me the blanks to fill out at once.
I did it, and that is how Phil's name came up as a
candidate. I myself mailed the indorsement, and
then took a petition and went around the town to
get the merchants to sign it in Phil's favor. The
first place I went to was Fink & Ditto's. Ditto was
over his books as usual, and when I told him what
I wanted he glared over his gold spectacles and said
it would do no good, because Ritchie was a Demo-
crat. Some days after this I was sitting in my
office with my back to the door, when suddenly I
heard some one right behind me. I had not heard
him enter, but it was Phil. 'Do you think I will
get appointed ?' The little fellow looked so handsome and so anxious that I told him that if he
would keep a secret I would tell him something.
He promised, and I told him I had a private advice
that he had been appointed. You should have
seen that boy. He fairly jumped and howled with
delight. His was not the only pleasure, for every
one in Somerset knew and liked the little chap, and

the appointment pleased them all. He went up for examination, and went through it as he did everything else. I have watched his career all through life, and there is just one little incident that shows the man. Everybody remembers when Early had driven Banks out of the valley and repulsed everybody who attempted to go up there. Grant got very tired of it, and sent word to Lincoln to send him some one to cope with Early. In a few days he received the following letter: 'I send you a man. There is not much of him, but he is the man you want.' That man was Phil Sheridan, and the way he hammered Early's forces is a matter of history. As a boy he was bright, polite, generous, and universally liked, and this is the story of the true way he got into his military career."

TOTALLY DEVOID OF FEAR.

The following little sample of the daring courage of Gen. Sheridan is told by a friend who knew him well : " At the close of the civil war, where he was the right-hand man of Grant, he did not stand parleying about old constitutional fooleries which had been overthrown by the side which made the war ; he did the truly valorous moral work of that war. He went to Louisiana, where there were murderers by hosts. He stopped at the principal hotel. A fellow jumped upon a table and told his fellow lunatics and blatherskites that he was going to kill Sheridan in a few minutes. Somebody went up to Sheridan's room and gave that information. " Well," said Sheridan, " let's go down and take a look at him." He walked down into the rotunda

of the St. Charles Hotel, where the man was still
going on.   Sheridan, surrounded by these murderers, looked calmly up at the fellow, whose attention
was presently called to the man he had just described as among the crows and kites.   The fellow
hopped down from his place, ran his head into the
crowd, fell down the back steps, and that was the
end of the matter.   This fellow was wanting to run
for the Senate or the Governorship, or Congress or
something.

SHERIDAN AT CEDAR CREEK.

Representative McKinley, of Ohio, who was a
major in the Union army, in talking of Gen. Sheridan
recently, vividly recalled the incidents when he led
the great charge after the disastrous defeat at
Cedar Creek.

"I was on Gen. Crook's staff," he said, "and
was posting some artillery under orders I had from
him, when Gen. Sheridan and his staff came riding
along the pike.   Sheridan had just came back from
Washington, where he had received his commission
as a major-general, and he knew nothing of the
disaster that had overtaken us.   He asked me where
Gen. Crook, was and I conducted him to headquarters.   The two generals retired a short distance
and engaged in close conversation.   Then Sheridan
decided that an immediate advance should be made
and the camps from which we had been driven be
recaptured.

" It was suggested that Gen. Sheridan should first
ride down the line, so that his presence might en-
courage the troops, and that they might know that

the General was once more among them. He had
on a new overcoat, such as we all wore, and this he
took off and handed to an orderly. Then a pair of
Major-General's epaulets were fastened upon his
shoulders, and in the full uniform of his rank at
the head of his staff he went dashing down the line.
What a scene that was! I never expect to witness
such another. The huzzas and shouts were deaf-
ening. His presence was as effective as two full
army corps. Sheridan said but little. Pointing to
our enemy's tents from which we had been driven,
he said :

"'Boys, those tents are ours ; we will sleep in
them to-night, will we not?'"

"A shout, 'That we will!' was the answer, and
a charge was made such as no power on earth could
have stayed. Sheridan looked the ideal soldier and
he had that peculiar power of inspiring every one
about him with his own confidence, as well as to
hold the love and affection of his men."

THE ROSSER EPISODE.

On the 4th of May, 1887, the *Times* of Winchester, Va., published the following letter from Gen.
Thomas L. Rosser, who had served with honor as
a cavalry officer in the Confederate army, to Major
Holmes Conrad, of Winchester :

"My DEAR MAJOR: I have seen it reported recently in the newspapers that Gen. P. H. Sheridan,
U.S.A., contemplates at an early day another ride
up the Shenandoah Valley. I had hoped that our
beautiful valley would never again be desecrated by
his footprints. Cold, cruel and brutal must be the

character of this soldier who fondly cherishes memories of the wild, wanton waste and desolation which his barbarous torch spread through the valley, laying in ashes the beautiful and happy homes of innocent women, young and helpless children and aged men, and who over these ruins boasted that 'now a crow cannot fly over this valley without carrying its rations.' Gen. Sheridan has done nothing since the war to atone for his barbarism during the war. We have not forgotten that during his reign in New Orleans, he asked that our fellow-citizens of Louisiana might be proclaimed banditti in order that he might set the dogs of war on them. I have forgiven the brave men of the Union armies whom I met in honorable battle, and who finally triumphed over us in the great struggle. Among them I can now name many of my warmest and truest and most prized friends. They are good and true to me and think none the less of us for having fought them. Indeed, they esteem him highest among us who fought them the hardest. Sheridan is not one of this kind, and never accorded to us that peace which Grant proclaimed. I now say to you, my dear major, and to our gallant comrades who are now in the valley, that I hope you will allow this man to make his triumphant ride up the valley in peace, but have him go like the miserable crow, carrying his rations with him.

"Yours truly,

"THOS. L. ROSSER."

This letter caused a great sensation, as it was written at the very time when Massachusetts sol-

diers were being entertained in Richmond, and was
a rare instance of a Southern man of high standing
waving the bloody shirt. The leading newspapers
North and South denounced Gen. Rosser's letter.
Gen. Sheridan had this to say of it:

"Rosser has not forgot the whaling I gave him
in the valley, and I am not surprised that he loses
his temper when he recalls it. Occasionally Rosser
would come across small detachments of our troops
and would swoop down on them. Finally it was
reported to me that Gen. Rosser had captured my
pack-train. This made me mad. Halting the entire
army right in the road, I galloped to the rear determined to settle Rosser. I found the train was
not captured, but was coming in considerably scattered and broken up. I told Torbert I wanted
Rosser cleaned out, and that if he could not do it I
would take his division and do it myself. I con-
cluded that I would remain and see the work performed, and so informed Torbert. The following
morning Torbert went after Rosser, whose brigade
was struck with an impetuosity that caused it to
scatter. We stripped the enemy of everything they
had captured; all their guns except one, which subsequently fell into our hands, and all their baggage,
including the personal effects of Rosser. It was a
regular frolic for our boys. Torbert pursued
Rosser a distance of twenty-five miles. He did not
trouble me further."

LITTLE PHIL IN BOSTON.

On the first day of February, 1888, Little Phil
visited Boston and held the town a willing captive.

It was his first visit to the Hub after succeeding Gen. Hancock as Commander-in-Chief of the military order of the Loyal Legion. The town unbent itself and made every effort to render his stay pleasant. He was dined as often as he could eat, and the Governor, his wife, the legislators, Mayor, city government, the military, the Back Bay aristocrat, the merchant, the Arab and the public school boy united to do him honor. The fact, of course, was that his name was brought into the list of possible Republican Presidential candidates, and the more that Gen. Sheridan was talked of as a candidate for President the more loudly echoed the expressions all the country over in his favor.

From the first, however, Sheridan was prompt to discourage the idea of putting him forward for Presidential honors. On the 19th of February the Washington agent of the Associated Press sought an interview with Gen. Sheridan for the purpose of ascertaining whether he would made an authoritative statement regarding his alleged candidacy. The soldier said he had never looked upon the newspaper articles with reference to the matter as anything more than the usual shooting around in the woods which had once or twice before in Presidential years brought his name up in that connection. " I never," he said, " have had the Presidential bee in my bonnet, and I don't intend to have it, for there is nothing that would induce me to leave the profession in which nearly forty years of my life have been spent to enter upon a civil career. So all talk about my being a Presidential candidate may as well end. I would not accept, no, not

under any circumstances. I do not want that or any other civil office.''

And so, still true to his first love, leal to the profession of arms, he chid away the ambition which, whispering at the portals of most men's ears, would have lured them to the pursuit of the bubble of civic renown.

A BRAVE AND DASHING SOLDIER.

Gen. Daniel Butterfield, an old companion-in-arms of Gen. Sheridan, spoke of him as follows : '' We had always been warm personal friends, and I have been very fond of him as a man outside of my warm admiration for his soldierly characteristics. He was a great soldier, a fighting soldier. As a leader he has never had a superior, in my judgment, in any army, at any time. I remember very vividly my first meeting with Gen. Sheridan. It was in the Chattanooga campaign, after the battle of Chickamauga, and I went out with the two corps which were sent from the Army of the Potomac. In the battle in front of Mission Ridge, when Sheridan led his division beyond the rifle-pits at the base and to the top of the ridge, being ordered only to take the rifle-pits, he first attracted Gen. Grant's notice as a leader. Grant had known him before the war, but the exhibition of Sheridan's peculiar bold dashing qualities as a soldier brought him into great prominence on that occasion.

'' The night after the battle I met Sheridan again, and the strong, positive nature of the man made a lasting impression on me. Sheridan had come up in front of Mission Ridge with his division, and I was with the advance of Gen. Osterhaus's division and Cruft's with Gen. Hooker on the crest of the Ridge and at the enemy's left. The converging of our two lines at right angles corralled, so to speak, a very large number of prisoners. Gen. Sheridan was much delighted with the situation, and vigorously pushed out with his division to pursue the retreating forces. Operations were suspended for the night when darkness came, and along about 10 o'clock I rode by accident through Gen. Sheridan's bivouac. I found him in front of a camp-fire pacing to and fro in a very earnest way, and he seemed rather displeased at something. 'General, you don't seem very much gratified after such a grand success as you have had to-day,' I remarked. 'What's the trouble?' His reply was characteristic of the man, and showed his dissatisfaction and impatience because darkness had prevented his vigorous forward movement.

"We were in Italy together after the Franco-Prussian war," continued Gen. Butterfield, "and his stories and recollection of past campaigns were exceedingly interesting and very vivid. It is to be regretted if these incidents of the war have not been written out by him or under his direction. The last time we were together was at the obsequies of the late Gen. Paez a few weeks ago. Gen. Sheridan put his hand on my shoulder and said: 'My dear fellow, I begin to realize that I'm not as strong and as tough as I used to be,' and then he asked if I thought it wise for him to ride in an open carriage. We took a closed carriage, and the troop of First Hussars were detailed as a special escort for us.

They were handsomely mounted, a fine-looking body of men. Gen. Sheridan looked at them very carefully, his eye sparkled with delight, and he said, turning to me : 'Butterfield, how I would like to be twenty-five years old and be one of those boys !'

"During our ride I referred to the earnest desire many of his old comrades in arms had to see him made President. He said : 'It would be very foolish in me, and aside from that it would kill me in sixty days. I know myself and my nature and the situation well enough to know that.' His was an earnest, truthful nature : there was no deceit in him."

BUFFALO BILL FOUGHT WITH HIM.

Buffalo Bill said, when asked if he knew Gen. Sheridan : "I know him well as an able and gallant officer and a true gentleman. He was like Gen. Boulanger, in that he inspired enthusiasm in all his men, and had their confidence and respect to an extent rarely witnessed. There was a certain romantic dash about him that made soldiers take a personal pride in being under his command, and you will hear men say proudly, 'I was with Phil Sheridan,' and then relate instances of his soldierly qualities. He was a tower of strength to our army during the war, which was weaker in able cavalry officers than the Confederate army. It, however, had no cavalry commander who was the equal of Sheridan. Personally, he was a man whom everybody loved who met him. He was genial and companionable. He had a remarkable memory, and, although he never posed as a book-worm, was well-

read, possessing a rare knowledge of military litera-
ture. He could write a great book on the art of
war. With me he will always be associated with
the pleasantest memories."

GEN. SHERMAN'S ESTIMATE.

Gen. William Tecumseh Sherman stated: "I
have frequently given my estimate of Gen. Sheridan—and the world knows what it is—what I
thought of his great abilities as a soldier and of his
character as a man. Sheridan's place in history
has long been established. His deeds and achievements, with those of Grant, Logan and other great
commanders of the civil war, are familiar house-
hold words throughout the land."

CHAUNCEY M. DEPEW'S RECOLLECTIONS.

Chauncey M. Depew said recently : "I did not
know Gen. Sheridan intimately, and I do not know
as I could give an estimate of his character that
would be of any value. Gen. Grant once told me,
however, in the course of a conversation, that he
regarded Gen. Sheridan as the greatest soldier of
the war, and that he did not think Sheridan's superior as a field officer could be found in the world.
Gen. Grant was certainly capable of judging such
matters, and his opinion of Sheridan will probably
be accepted by the country at large. I have met
Gen. Sheridan a good many times at dinners and
other places. My acquaintance with him was very
friendly and pleasant. I found in him a jolly, un-
affected man, full of good stories himself and fond
of hearing them from others. He was in no sense a

partisan, and I believe he took very little interest in politics. I think it doubtful if he voted at all of late years. We are more than ever forcibly reminded that the heroes of the war are fast disappearing from view, and that we are going rapidly into an age that has no actual recollection of that great conflict. Sherman and Rosecrans are about the only ones left among the more prominent commanders on the Union side. All of the commanders of the Army of the Potomac and Army of the Cumberland are gone. Three-fourths of the voting population of the country have become voters since the war closed, and one-third of our voters were born since that memorable conflict began. It is hard for me to realize it, but to the majority of our people the war is simply a history, they have no actual recollection of it. It is remarkable, too, the ignorance of the younger generation of the events oi the war—where the great battles were fought, who commanded, etc. They know as little about it as they do of the Mexican war and the Revolution."

OTHER TRIBUTES TO THE SOLDIER.

Major-Gen. Daniel E. Sickles said : "He was a great soldier. Gen. Grant told me he regarded Sheridan as the greatest soldier of his time. Von Moltke, with whom he spent some time at headquarters during the Franco-Prussian war as his guest, had a very high opinion of him. Among the most serious mistakes made by the Emperor Napoleon III. was when he refused to receive Gen. Sheridan at headquarters, saying he didn't want any

foreign officers there.   Sheridan's sympathies were
naturally with the French, I think, and the Emperor would have got many precious hints from him.
Sheridan would have told him how to operate on
the German communications, which the French
never knew how to cut or disturb.

"Sheridan's character impressed itself readily
upon his command.   He gave to his men an intrep-
idity, a confidence, an audacity like his own, which
enabled him to get a great deal more work out of
ten thousand than another commander would get
from twenty thousand.   His presence with a command fairly doubled its strength.   And it may be
said of Sheridan, as well as of Sherman and Grant,
that, apart from their military genius, much of
their success was due to their unbounded confidence in volunteer soldiers.   That confidence was
reciprocated by the soldiers and made them invincible.   His military career was remarkable.   He
was a humble lieutenant when the war began, and
in four years he carved his way with his sword to
the position of, perhaps the most brilliant of all the
commanders.   Of course, in saying this, I detract
nothing from the reputation of Sherman and Hancock, whose genius was equally great with Sheridan's, but of a different temperament.   Sheridan's
peculiar genius was shown most most forcibly at
Winchester and Five Forks.   Those two combats
mark him as a tactician and leader of the highest
order.

"Sheridan's character as a soldier is summed np
in one of his famous phrases at Five Forks—'Push
things!'"

SOLDIER AND CITIZEN.

GENERAL SCOFIELD'S LOVING WORDS.

"I DEEPLY regret the loss the army has sustained, and I have lost a very dear comrade and lifelong friend. Sheridan and I were at West Point together. He entered the Academy in 1848, and I came the following year. We graduated in the same class, however, in 1853, as did also General James B. McPherson, who was killed in 1864 at Atlanta while repulsing a sortie. John B. Hood, who rose to the rank of a general in the Confederate service, was likewise a fellow-classmate of ours.

"All four of us were warm friends through all our lives. For Sheridan I always entertained a deep affection, a sentiment I knew he returned Mc Pherson cherished the same feelings for Sheridan and myself as we did for him. Though Hood was on the other side we, who remained in the service of the United States government, only regretted that his different ideas of duty had separated us from a pleasant comrade.

"Regarding General Sheridan's military career, I do not know that I can say anything to add to his fame. Both Grant and Sherman have taken occasion in their memoirs to speak of Sheridan in the highest terms, and I consider the estimates of these two chief commanders are just, and their praise well deserved. Grant knew Sheridan best, and his tribute to his gallant subordinate is one of the many touches which have revealed to us the true character and generous nature of the greatest soldier of his time. To Sherman my dead friend was best known as a young officer, full of dash and vigor, yet he saw enough of him to known that Philip H. Sheridan was no common soldier.

" To me Sheridan was always the beau ideal of a true soldier and a really great commander. He is one of the few American officers who attained high and responsible rank through his natural force of character and his military genius. He was a marked man, even at West Point, for he displayed at that early stage of his military life the same sterling qualities which snbsequently made him a prominent character in our national history.

" As a cadet he was noticeable among his fellows for devotion to drill and the routine of study. No lesson was distasteful to him, no branch was slighted or neglected. He took great pleasure in the practical studies and was as fond of the manual of arms as the handling of field guns. In the riding school and the cavalry evolutions Sheridan was in his element, for he loved horses. In the saddle he was at home, and he became a proficient swordsman. While learning the duties of a soldier Sheridan was invariably cheerful and light-hearted, being fond of mischief at times, though he never overstepped the rules of discipline. He and I were chums, and our friendship was never marred or shaken in after-years. As I remember him he was a young man whom everybody at the Point liked, and he was a favorite with the professors.

"Sheridan was a very impulsive man, and rather quick, if not hasty, in his anger. It was his nature

and not his fault, for he could not help it, though
he always strove to overcome the defect. But however quick and hasty he might be, he was always
ready and prompt to make the most generous
amends. While he was in command of a division
in the West he was very harsh one day in the treatment of an unfortunate Colonel who was in temporary command of a brigade. Sheridan fell into a
fierce rage, and in his hot anger used language
which the Colonel felt compelled to resent, being
as passionate a man as Sheridan. The moment he
uttered his words of resentment Sheridan's anger
cooled off as suddenly as it had risen. On the
instant he held out his hand to the astonished
Colonel, saying, " You are right, and I am wrong.
I beg your pardon!"

"From that day Sheridan had no better friend
than this Colonel, who never forgot the incident or
the lesson, though he himself rose to the rank of a
general.

I was not present in the Shenandoah Valley dur-
Sheridan's famous campaign, but I have had the
scenes in the battles of Winchester and Cedar Creek
vividly described to me by competent eye-witnesses.
From these descriptions I became convinced that
those important victories were not only gained by
his military skill, but were due in a great measure
to his soldierly qualities and his personal magnetism and electrical influence over his troops.

" Every officer I have ever met, whatever rank
they might have held, who served under Sheridan
in the West or the East, have shown by their language that they honored and loved him. That is

something you cannot say of every man who wore the shoulder-straps of a general.

"How I wish Philip H. Sheridan could have been longer spared to his country and to the army, for he was a great man, a faithful public servant and a soldier of heroic mould. American history will record his services as those of a man who always sought to do his duty wherever he found it, and will speak of him as his career deserves.

Gen. Crook said :

"General Sheridan and I were classmates at West Point. He came there a somewhat raw country youth, like the most of us, and I cannot recall anything that in those days marked him as probably destined for an extrordinary career of any kind. I would say that he appreciated his good fortune in having obtained a nomination to a cadetship, and realized the necessity of hard study and a clean record to take him through his classes to the desired commission. He stood well with his fellow cadets, though possessing none of that brilliancy that goes to the making of the pets or idols of the corps. He was a quiet, civil, little fellow, industrious at his lessons, attentive at his recitations, and careful in the many little things that go to the fixing of a cadet's standing for obedience and discipline. After graduation we were members of the same regiment, but I really saw little of him till the war was well advanced. Concerning his qualities as a commander I am not presumptuous enough to suppose that I can add anything to the much that has been said, and on the whole well said, of him, both as a leader of cavalry and as an independent commander. Popular opinion has associated his name with that of Grant and Sherman as the pre-eminent soldiers on the Federal side of the civil war, and this opinion has been confirmed by those at home and abroad who have made the art of war a study. He was liked in the service by all ranks and at all times, both as a man and an officer, and that to my mind is as good an evidence as could be of his manly and soldierly qualities. His name is a bright one on the roll of the army of the United States, and I believe that he earned and deserved all the fame and fortune that came to him. He made his own way in the profession, and so far as I know he never stood in the light of any of his com. Forks.

General W. S. Rosecrans said : "When I is to command of the small Army of the Mississ!y in Sheridan was colonel of a Michigan regiment no that army. I knew him well and watched his care reer closely. He was a hard fighter, stubborn and unyielding. At Booneville he won his first star, and at Stone River another, and so on, and every success that has come to him has been earned. With all his stubbornness and dash he was prudent, cautious, a good provider for his army, and was always careful to know the topography of the country in which he was operating. And then he was prompt to take his troops into action under heavy firing. There are many men who do unpleasant things, even though a duty, hesitatingly. They wait and consider and doubt. Sheridan, on the instant, went straight for the mark ; no delays, no doubts. He was indeed a great general, and the country will deeply mourn his loss."

Representative Spinola, of New York, said: "I first met Sheridan in 1862, in the Army of the Potomac. He was then in charge of the cavalry forces, and his qualities as a soldier endeared him to every man in the rank and file of the army. He was looked up to with the highest degree of respect by everybody as one of the first fighters in the army. Since the war my connection with General Sheridan was purely social, and it has always been very pleasant. It could not have been otherwise, owing to his genial qualities and the fact that he followed the dictates of a great big generous heart."

Inspector-General Baird, who was graduated from anything Point Academy three years before Genebly Sheridan, and who from the first years of the I wo was intimately associated with him in the army, have pressed the opinion that General Sheridan was really the equal of any soldier in history.

Senator Reagan of Texas, Postmaster-General of the Confederacy, said: "I think the country has lost a very able officer."

Major-General C. M. Wilcox, who commanded a division in A. P. Hill's corps, Army of Northern Virginia, said: "The only time I met Sheridan during the war was at Appomattox, when General Gordon and myself received him with a flag of truce. He came to our line to inquire whether it were true that negotiations were pending for Lee's surrender. To Gordon's affirmative answer, he said, 'Well, then, let us draw off our forces, that not another man may be hurt,' which was done."

Representative Wheeler, of Alabama, said the first time he met Sheridan was under a flag of truce in 1862. "He told me," said General Wheeler, "all about his promotion, and expressed his determination to deserve it. In the course of that interview I was struck by the strength of purpose exhibited by him."

Representative Forney of Alabama said : "I was opposed to him at Appomattox. There he rendered greater service than any other man. On the 7th we had whipped them (the Union forces), but he came around us on the 8th and forced us to surrender, for otherwise we would have reached Lynchburg, and securing fresh supplies would have been able to have held out. He turned our right and forced us to evacuate the work at Petersburg Five Forks. He captured the last railroad and forced us to leave. He was afterward in our rear and finally in our front. Altogether as a lieutenant under General Grant he had no superior and there could have been no better."

Representative Chandler of Georgia, who was a colonel in the Confederate army, said he regarded General Sheridan as a very gallant man and a superior military chieftain. Certainly he was a very distinguished soldier, a man of unquestionably soldierly qualities, and as conscientious as any man.

Secretary Endicott said : "General Sheridan's death is a great loss to the army and this department. I mean as a practical, energetic man of affairs. He had a wide experience, gathered during an active military life. He knew and understood all conditions of army life in all parts of the country, and of the people with whom our soldiers have to deal, including the Indians, in whom he took peculiar interest. He was wise and sagacious, and his judgment was marked by readiness in decision and guided by shrewd common sense. He had so long held high command, and had been attended by such success, that he felt a confidence in his administration of affairs which was rarely at fault. I always found him most reasonable and ready to look at all sides of a question, and for a man of such impulses most open to conviction. As a soldier he, of course, stands quite by himself, differing with a marked and intense individuality from all our distinguished soldiers. As a cavalry soldier he was preëminent. The rapidity of his movements, the energy with which he inspired officers and men, his unerring instincts on the battle-field led necessarily to great success, that was well deserved. He was very interesting and entertaining in social intercourse: he had a fund of anecdote, a variety of information that often was very instructive. His experiences in Europe, when he accompanied the German army to France in 1870, were varied and very interesting.

Secretary Fairchild said that he had become acquainted with General Sheridan since his arrival in Washington, and had taken a great liking to him from the first.

Postmaster General Dickinson said: "He was a great general, and had the simplicity of manners which always accompanies true greatness. He attached men to him with an affection in which there was something of peculiar tenderness. No man was more universally loved, and the places that knew him and all at the capital will miss him sadly."

All the leading Senators and members of Congress spoke in terms of admiration for General Sheridan as a soldier and as a man, those who had long known him extolling him highly and all echoing the sentiment of sorrow for his death.

CLASSMATES' RECOLLECTIONS.

BLOWS WITH A COMRADE WHICH COST HIM ONE YEAR'S SUSPENSION.

"GENERAL SHERIDAN and myself were classmates at West Point in 1849," said Assistant Adjutant General Thomas M. Vincent, " and among other members of that class was W. R. Terrill, killed at the battle of Perryville, Ky., October 8, 1862, who was indirectly the cause of General Sheridan's being set back a year in his class at the Academy. During the first encampment of the cadets in 1849, Sheridan, A. V. Kautz—now colonel of the Eighth Infantry—and myself were tentmakers for two months, and naturally were brought into very close communication. There were fifty-two members in our class, which graduated in 1853, General Sheridan standing 34.

" While at West Point he was always known for his diffidence, and in after-life he was never obtrusive, no matter what the conditions or circumstances might be. He was always sociable, however, and a great favorite in circles in which he mingled. After he located permanently at Washington, Kautz, Sheridan and myself were always very friendly, from the fact that we were all Buckeyes, and the General was always well disposed toward any one from his native State."

Brigadier-General Thomas H. Rogers, commanding the department of Dakota, was at West Point at the same time with General Sheridan, but was two classes lower, as he did not enter the Academy until 1851.

"I remember as well as if it happened to-day," said the General, "the difficulty between Cadet Phil Sheridan and Cadet Corporal W. B. Terrill, who was a native of Virginia. He was considerably larger and taller than Sheridan, but both were noted among the cadets as being very game fellows. They had words between them about some matter, I don't recall exactly what it was, but it culminated in Sheridan striking the Virginian as the parade roll was being called for dinner and the battalion was drawn up in line.

"When the trouble broke out, caused by some remark of Terrill's, without hesitation as to consequences, Sheridan retaliated with a blow, but this was as far as the difficulty went. Both cadets were separated, and Sheridan was placed in arrest for his infraction of discipline. That blow cost him one year's suspension, and he was sent home to his residence in Ohio. There was no effort made by either of the principals to come together and settle the difficulty with another fight, and afterward they became good friends.

"His qualities, dash, and impetuosity endeared him to General Grant, who always spoke of him in the highest terms as a brave officer, and one in whom

CAPTURE OF LOOKOUT MOUNTAIN.

he had the most implicit confidence. Sheridan possessed personal magnetism which made him the idol of his command, and his impulsiveness was in direct contrast with the phlegmatic temperament of Grant, who was beloved by his troops for his plain, unassuming manners. Undoubtedly General Sheridan was one of the greatest generals that ever lived."

HIS CHICAGO FRIENDS.

MANY VIEWS OF HIS REMARKABLE EXCELLENCES— BUT ONE VOICE OF PRAISE.

THE number of old soldiers in Chicago who served under Sheridan in the days when he made his brilliant record is comparatively few. Sheridan's soldiers, with a few exceptions, were recruited from New York, Pennsylvania, Virginia, and other eastern States. Among those now residing in Chicago who saw service by the side of "Little Phil" is General A. C. McClurg, who served as assistant adjutant of the Twenty-second Army corps under General McCook.

General McClurg said : "If asked what seemed to constitute his distinguishing characteristic I should say that it was his faculty of always holding himself in readiness for action. And yet he would impress a new comer as being precisely the opposite. He looked anything but a hard-working officer. He always acted as if he was a man with plenty of leisure, without any of the cares and responsibilities of life to mar his serenity. The fact

was that he always knew the exact situation, down
to the finest detail. He had the faculty of doing
everything through his subordinates, and had them
in hand so well that mistakes never happened."

"I first met Sheridan," said General L. P. Brad-
ley, "in the country around Nashville. He was
one of the most painstaking commanders I ever
knew. He never risked a life unless the risk was
absolutely necessary. In war his foresight was wonderful. Great good sense was his distinguishing
characteristic. He was always occupied in caring
for his troops, and to this care he owed the efficiency of his command.

"I remember, at a dinner which was given to him
by the Loyal Legion on March 6, 1882, how he
then said: 'People think I am·rash and reckless.
I say that there never was an officer more prudent
than I. I encamped my men well, watched their
rations and comforts, and when we fought the
enemy I gave them the confidence of victory from
my knowledge of the enemy and my confidence in
the men.' I indorse every word of what he said
then. Such was Sheridan in war."

Alexander E. Stevenson was Inspector-General on
General Sheridan's staff from December, 1862, till
November, 1863. His position enabled him to observe closely the methods of Sheridan during two
of the most critical periods of his military career,
the battles of Stone River and Chickamauga.

" General Sheridan's foresight and extraordinary
energy were what made him great as a commander,"
said General Stevenson. I don't suppose there ever
was a general with greater power of electrifying

his men. In camp he was a most modest man, quiet, unassuming, and easy of approach. But let something go wrong when his division was moving, and the contrast was astonishing. Profanity was the climax of Sheridan's enthusiasm in great crises, and it always carried its point. His men became like himself, irresistible. Their remarkable affection for him is proof that he never was brutal."

Among his old Chicago friends "Little Phil" is membered as one of the worst presiding officers ever seen in a deliberative body. This was a rare tribute to the man's modesty. He was so shy, retiring and modest that the faces of those who knew him well were enough to put him out and embarrass him greatly.

General Sheridan loved to see a close finish on the turf. He attended every meeting at Washington Park except the last one, and was always present on Derby day. He liked to go into the judges' stand, and on several occasions he acted as a judge to the entire satisfaction of everybody. He was president of the Washington Park Club.

HOW THE GREAT SOLDIER FOUGHT THE BATTLE OF FIVE FORKS.

THE crowning point in Sheridan's brilliant military career was the battle of Five Forks. There his signal victory forced the retreat of Lee and his army from their intrenched positions around Richmond and Petersburg, and was followed by the surrender of Appomattox and the end of the civil war.

Five Forks was a position on the extreme right of
Lee's defensive line, and somewhat detached from
it. Its strategic value was incalculable in importance, since the loss of it would at once leave the
Army of Northern Virginia open to attack upon
its lines of communication ; and thus the precipi
tate retreat of that army from its strongly fortified
places would become unavoidable. The spot takes
its name from the fact that it is the point where the
Dinwiddie, Scott's, the White Oak, Ford's Church,
and another road concentrate. It had been occupied by Pickett's infantry and all the cavalry of
Lee's army. While it was indispensable to Lee, it
had already been recognized by Grant as of equal
importance to him in his offensive movements then
to begin.

It was on March 29, 1865, after an extended interview at City Point with President Lincoln, that
Gen. Grant moved his headquarters to the centre of
his line in front of Petersburg. His forces were at
this time disposed as follows, from right to left:
Weitzel in front of Richmond, north of the James
River ; Parke and Wright holding the works in
front of Petersburg ; Ord extending south to the
intersection of the Vaughn road and Hatcher's Run ;
Humphrey's left reaching beyond Dabney's saw-
mill ; Warren on the extreme left, and covering the
front as far as the intersection of the Vaughn road
and the Boydton plank road ; while Sheridan, with
the whole cavalry corps, was at Dinwiddie Court
House. The weather was very cloudy, and as the
day drew to a close rain began to fall. During that
night and the next day the storm continued with

but little interruption. The ground was soft, and
the rain soon soaked it into greater softness, so that
by the evening of the 30th the whole country became, as it were, one vast bed of mushy quicksand,
in which the horses of the cavalry and artillery
sank almost to their bellies.

This condition was, in a measure, favorable to the
Confederates, as it enabled them to secure more
time to complete all their preparations to receive an
attack which was inevitable, and, therefore, the
more successfully to resist it. The roads had become streams of water, and it was with extreme
difficulty that the artillery and trains of Grant's
forces could move upon them. It was this situation
of the roads that had prevented Gen. Grant from
sending a corps of infantry to reinforce Sheridan on
the 30th, and when the latter rode into Grant's
headquarters on the morning of that day he so informed him.

From the inception of the movement, Sheridan
understood its importance as bearing on the ter-
mination of the war, and gave no thought to himself. No hardship or effort was too great for him
to undergo. He was here, there, and everywhere
about the field of the coming battle, his keen military eye and sound judgment ever on the alert.
Gen. Grant told him at the interview in his tent
that he wished him to feel the enemy's strength
next day, and, if possible, to seize Five Forks. As
the two generals sat together the rain continued to
pour in torrents. "General," said Sheridan as he
rose to go, "I will execute your plans to morrow

though the elements and all the powers of the Confederacy stand in the way."

The weather continued cloudy and rainy on the 31st, and Sheridan reported to Grant that the Confederates had been busily engaged intrenching at Five Forks and to the west of that point for the distance of a mile; and it was evident that a determined effort would be made there by Lee to protect his right flank. Gen. Grant, anticipating an attack upon his left, held by Warren, had cautioned the latter to be on his guard against it. An advance of the Fifth Corps on the White Oak road developed a strong force occupying it, and before going very far this corps met with a determined and vigorous resistance which brought it to a halt. The fighting which ensued was fast and furious, and reflected great credit on the contending troops. Gen. Warren distinguished himself by his coolness and gallantry, and evinced in many ways those fine soldierly qualities of which he was undoubtedly possessed. In the mean time Sheridan, in accordance with his instructions of the day before, had moved upon Five Forks, and had encountered a little north of Dinwiddie Court House a strong force of infantry and cavalry. This day, Sheridan has often said jocularly, was the liveliest day of his life, as he had to fight infantry and cavalry with cavalry alone.

The conditions of the problem did not, however, daunt his intrepid spirit. Sheridan never seemed so well pleased as when fighting under difficulties. His martial faculties then had full play, and he revelled in the task of surmounting and overcoming the odds against him. On this occasion he hurled his cavalry against the Confederate infantry, with undaunted heart, and when confronted at important points by the enemy's cavalry, equally as intrepid as his own, he met it with an onset that was almost invincible. He informed a staff officer of Grant's who had been sent to observe his movements, that he was concentrating his forces on the high ground just north of Dinwiddle, and that he would hold that position. At the same time he requested the staff officer to go to Gen. Grant and urge him to send up the Sixth Army Corps. He specified this corps because it had been with him in the Shenandoah Valley and understood his methods of fighting. He was informed that the position occupied by the Sixth Corps precluded its being sent to his assistance, but that the Fifth Corps would reach him by daylight the next morning. This was a busy night. Staff officers were rushing about all night, carrying orders from one headquarters to another, getting information, and hurrying up the movements of the troops that were to take part in this supreme effort to destroy Lee's army and bring the long war to a close.

Gen. Warren, who had accompanied Crawford's division of his corps, reached and reported in person to Sheridan at 11 A.M. In less than one hour afterward Gen. Babcock of Grant's staff arrived and said to Sheridan : " Gen. Grant directs me to say to you that if in your judgment the Fifth Corps would do better under one of the division commanders, you are authorized to relieve Gen. War· ren, and order him to report to him (Grant) at headquarters." The reason was nothing more than a belief, prevailing at Grant's headquarters, that Warren was not sufficiently energetic and aggressive. It was most unjust to Warren, who had signalized his loyalty, his courage, and his ability on the Gettysburg battlefield. Sheridan's only reply to Babcock, when he received this order, was that he hoped such a step would not become necessary.

The Confederate earthworks ran along the White Oak road, and were something over a mile and a half in length, with a southerly line at right angles with the main line, extending about three hundred yards from it. Sheridan had dismounted his cavalry in front of these earthworks, and had directed Warren to attack the angle by wheeling to the left, and to sweep down by a westward movement and come in the rear of the enemy's intrenched position. As soon as the cavalry should hear the firing of Warren's infantry, it was to make a vigorous assault upon the Confederate front. When all had been arranged, Sheridan awaited the attack of the Fifth Corps, but, for some unexplained reason, the movement was slow, and the formation for it seemed to be delayed and to drag. It was then that the ardent nature of this consummate soldier became impatient, and he appeared to be consumed with anxiety. Those who have been led by historians to believe that Sheridan was of a rash, impetuous nature—a man governed wholly by his impulses—have been misinformed. The truth is that he was impetuous only where impetuosity was needed. He was never rash in any military move-

BATTLE OF GETTYSBURG.

ment. He felt the importance of prompt action at this stage of the battle, and in every possible way appealed for it ; he dismounted from his horse and walked to and fro, with knit brow and troubled mien ; he seemed overwhelmed by the tardiness of his subordinates. He understood the consequences of delays in their bearing on the fate of armies, and he knew how dangerous they are. No wonder, then, that on this occasion he was so deeply troubled.

It was not until 4 o'clock that the troops got into position and everything was in readiness for the assault on Pickett's line. When a staff officer rode up to Sheridan to report the position of the command, he found him standing with one arm thrown across his saddle, in no pleasant frame of mind. "Everything is ready, you say?" answered Sheridan eagerly. "Thank God! It may be too late! Order them forward at once, and we'll take our chances and win, come what may." Saying this, he sprang into the saddle.

Very soon after the men of Ayres's division encountered a heavy fire on their left and were forced to change their course to a more westward direction. Moving rapidly forward through a dense wood and over the soft boggy ground, they received a severe shock from the angle, and fell back in great confusion. This was the moment when Sheridan rose to the full significance of the situation. Dashing into the midst of the broken and dismayed lines, he cried out : "Where is my battle flag?" Seizing the staff, he wrenched it from the hand of the sergeant who carried it, and waving the crimson and white standard above his head he cheered and encouraged the men. The whizzing of bullets and bursting of shells was terrific. The battle flag was riddled ; the sergeant who had borne it was killed ; staff officers were wounded, and many horses were knocked down. Nothing daunted by this leaden storm, Sheridan galloped from point to point of the line, waving his standard, threatening, exhorting, swearing, beseeching the men to stand firm and hurl back the foe. He was the very impersonation of courage ; the incarnation of battle. His example was infectious. Ayres and his officers shared with him the exposure and the effort. The veterans of the ranks soon reformed their lines, and with wild cheers rushed forward and carried the earthworks. Sweeping the way clear before them, they killed, captured, or put to flight every man in their way. That day Sheridan rode Rienzi, the gallant horse that had been presented to him by the people of Michigan. Arriving near the angle, Sheridan spurred him on, and with a bound he landed his rider again in the midst of victory and a long line of prisoners, who, having thrown down their arms, were seeking safety behind their breastworks. Gen. Horace Porter, who was present, states that "some of these prisoners called out: 'Whar do you want us all to go ?' Then Sheridan's rage turned to humor, and he had a running talk with the Johnnies as they filed past : 'Go right over there,' he cried, pointing to the rear, 'get right along now. Drop your guns, you'll never need them any more. You'll be safe over there. Are there any more of you ? We want every one of you fellows.' " Nearly 1500 were captured at the angle.

While these decisive movements were taking place on the right, the cavalry in front, under Merritt, Custer, and Devin, had gallantly gone over the earthworks, and, promptly carrying out Sheridan's order, had captured a battery of artillery, many prisoners, and swept away everything that opposed them in their terrible outslaught. After the seizure of the angle, Gen. Sheridan made his way to the westward of the Fort road, and here again threw all the energy of his nature into the effort to destroy finally the forces of Pickett. He relieved Warren of his command and placed Griffin in the head of the Fifth Corps, and expecting that Lee would attack him on the following morning with fresh troops, he busily engaged in collecting together his detached commands and strengthening his position.

As Gen. Horace Porter, who witnessed the struggle in all its details, says : " Sheridan had that day fought one of the most interesting technical battles of the war, almost perfect in conception, brilliant in execution, strikingly dramatic in its incidents, and productive of immensely important results." The immediate effect was to determine Grant to order an advance along his entire front on the following day. Lee, recognizing the extent of the disaster, was forced to call Longstreet to the south side of the James, and to make dispositions for the retreat of his shattered and demoralized troops. The successful assault of Grant's columns on the following day, the desperate resistance of Lee, and the retreat and final surrender of the Army of Northern Virginia at Appomattox, were the legitimate outcome of this marvellous victory of Sheridan at Five Forks.

———

MR. PLUMB'S REMINISCENCE OF THE GENERAL.

SENATOR PLUMB said : "I always think of Sheridan in connection with one conversation I had with him.

"'General,' said I, 'you were in the West before you came East. What was your opinion of the Army of the Potomac? You remember it was criticised about that time as not doing its share of the work.'

"'Oh, the Army of the Potomac was all right,' said Sheridan. 'The trouble was the commanders never went out to lick anybody, but always thought first of keeping from getting licked.'

"Sheridan came East when the cavalry of the Army of the Potomac was not in good condition, and Grant gave him the task of reorganizing it and raising its efficiency. He had worked away some time when Meade sent him over the Rappahannock on a reconnoissance. Sheridan came back and in making his verbal report referred to a brush he had with Stuart's cavalry.

"'Never mind Stuart,' said Meade, interrupting, 'he will do about as he pleases anyhow. Go on and tell me what you discovered about Lee's forces.'

"That made Sheridan mad, and he retorted : 'I can thrash Stuart any day.'

Meade repeated the remark to Grant, who queried : ' Why didn't you tell him to do it?'

"Not long after, sure enough, Sheridan got an order to cross the river, engage Stuart, and clean him out.

" 'I knew I could whip him,' said Sheridan, 'if I could only get him where he could not fall back on Lee's infantry. So I thought the matter over, and to draw him on started straight for Richmond. We moved fast, and Stuart dogged us right at our heels. We kept on a second day straight for Richmond, and the next morning found Stuart in front of us just where we wanted him. He had marched all night and got around us. Then I rode him down. I mashed his command and broke up his divisions and regiments and brigades, and the poor fellow himself was killed there. Right there, Senator, I resisted the greatest temptation of my life. There lay Richmond before us, and there was nothing to keep us from going in. It would have cost five or six hundred lives, and I could not have held the place, of course. But I knew that the moment it was learned at the North that a Union army was in Richmond, then every bell would ring, and I should have been the hero of the hour. I could have gone in and burned and killed right and left. But I had learned this thing—that our men knew what they were about. I had seen them come out of a fight in which only a handful were killed, discontented, mad clear through, because they knew an opportunity had been lost, or a sacrifice, small as it was, had been needlessly made ; and I had seen them come out good-natured, enthusiastic, and spoiling for more, when they had left the ground so thickly covered with dead that you could have crossed it on the bodies alone. They realized that, notwithstanding the terrible sacrifice, the object gained had been worth it. They would have followed me, but they would have known as well as I that the sacrifice was for no permanent advantage.'

"That," continued Senator Plumb, "exhibits the man and the commander. He aimed to win and keep the confidence of his men, and he did it. He fought for results and not for glory."

A companion in arms relates the following:

After the battle of Cedar Creek, President Lincoln and Secretary Stanton agreed that Sheridan should receive some special recognition for the great exploit. They promoted him to be a Major-General in the regular army, and when the commission was made out the President decided that it should be sent to the General, who still lay near Cedar Creek, by an unusual messenger. I was selected for this agreeable duty.

From Washington to Harper's Ferry I went by rail, but there it was necessary to have an escort. Starting early in the morning and riding all day with no other interruptions than were caused by the occasional appearance of Mosby's cavalry here and there on our flank, it was about ten at night before we reached the General's stopping-place. He had gone to bed, but was waked up to receive the important document. The speeches on the occasion were brief, but they were to the purpose. Sheridan was not displeased with the transaction.

The next morning the General took me on foot through his camp, and as we went among the regiments and brigades, and greeted old acquaintances on every hand, I was everywhere struck with the manifestations of personal attachment to Sheridan. I had not seen anything like it in either of our great armies. Grant, Sherman, Thomas, all moved among their troops with every sign of respect and confidence on the part of the men ; but in Sheridan's camp it was quite different. They seemed to regard · him more as a boy regards the father he believes in, relies on, and loves, than as soldiers are wont to regard their commander. Finally, as we were completing our morning's tour and had got nearly back to headquarters, I said to him : "General, how is this ? These men seem to have a special affection for you, more than I have ever seen displayed toward any other officer. What is the reason ?"

"Well," said he, "I think I can tell you. I always fight the front rank myself. I was long ago convinced that it would not do for a commanding general to stay in the rear of the troops and carry on a battle with paper orders, as they do in the Army of the Potomac. These men all know that where it is hottest, there I am, and they like it, and that is the reason they like me."

THE GENERAL'S LONGEST SPEECH.

AN ADDRESS TO VETERANS THAT WENT TO THEIR HEARTS.

THE longest speech ever delivered by General Sheridan was made at the Creston reunion of the veterans of Southwest Iowa and Northwest Missouri. There were at least ten thousand veterans present, in addition to thousands of other persons. The enthusiasm for Sheridan was overwhelming, and contrary to custom he had at last yielded to the importunities of the veterans and made a speech that went direct to every old soldier's heart. It was wholly impromptu and characteristic, and was as follows:

"Comrades :—I came here to-day to see you and talk with you and shake hands with you, while Colonel Carr and others, you know, came here to make eloquent addresses for you to listen to. I think he has been too eulogistic of me in his remarks. It is true that I fought in almost everybody's army from Pea Ridge to Appomattox, and although I fought with cavalry and infantry and on every line of operation, and always had to change and take new men on new lines, I was very successful. I went through all the grades they had in the volunteer service, and then I commenced and went through all the grades in the regular service, and the date of every commission that I have is the date of a battle.

"Now I want to say to you, comrades, that I am indebted to the private in the ranks for all this credit that has come to me. ˙[Applause, long and continued.] He was the man who did the fighting, and the man who carried the musket is the greatest hero of the war in my opinion. I was nothing but an agent; I knew how to take care of men. I knew what a soldier was worth, and I knew how to study the country so as to put him in right ; I knew how to put him in a battle when one occurred, but I was

BATTLE OF CHAPIN'S FARM.

simply the agent to take care of him, and he did the work. Now, comrades, these are common-sense things, and I can't say them in very flowery language, but they are true, nevertheless, and they are true not of me alone, but of everybody else. It is to the common soldier that we are indebted for any credit to us.

" Now, I am glad to see you here to-day, gentlemen, and I am glad to be with you on his occasion. There are many men here to-day who served in the field with me, and it is a great pleasure to me to find them out, and they have been very kindly in their remarks to me. While they were with me I certainly did all I could for them. I often lay awake planning for their welfare, and I never killed a man unnecessarily. One great trouble with men who command troops is that they kill men unnecessarily. You may kill as many men as you choose if you give them an equivalent for the loss Men do not like to be killed for nothing; they do not like to have their heads rammed against a stone wall unless for some good results. These are points I made during the war. Whenever I took men into a battle I gave them victory as the result of the engagement, and that was always satisfactory."

GEN. SHERIDAN WAS LASSOED.

According to Col. Archer Mason, Gen. Sheridan once had his life saved in an odd way. Col. Mason's regiment was once giving the General a reception at the California Theatre. Sheridan was standing

in the wings, peeping out beside the curtain at the
audience, when he suddenly pointed to one of the
musicians, and asked Mason :

" Isn't that man named Blyth ? "

On being told that he was, he asked to have him
brought up on the stage at once. After a cordial
greeting, which almost wrung the musician's hand
off, Sheridan said :

"I have good reason to remember Mr. Blyth, for
he saved my life for me once. It was when I was a
young cavalry officer, fighting the Indians. Blyth
was a private in my troop. One day we were having a hand-to-hand set-to with the Indians, and one
of the red devils had just shot at me with a revolver.
I had my sabre very close to his neck when another
Indian threw his lasso around my neck, and in
another instance I would have been trampled under
the feet of the horses. But Blyth, who was close
beside me, cut the rope with his sabre and saved my
life."

SHERIDAN'S FIRST VICTORY.

In Whitelaw Reid's " Ohio in the War " there
are several good stories about Sheridan's boyhood.
One how he pluckily stuck on a vicious horse when
only five years of age, and rode it after excellent
horsemen had failed.

This was Sheridan's first victory.

Another time Patrick McNanly, Sheridan's school
teacher at Somerset, tried to punish Phil because
some boy had thrown a bucket of water over him.

Phil ran home, the teacher chasing him until Phil's dog Rover treed the teacher and kept him there. McNanly begged Phil to call off the dog, for it was bitter cold, but the boy would not. Mr. Sheridan came out, and as Phil said he had not thrown any water, the dog was not called off until the teacher had promised not to "lick" Phil.

This was the first surrender to Sheridan.

A good sample of the way Sheridan had of dealing with refractory "natives" during the war is told by Colonel Newhall. It occurred at Prince Edward's Court House. A Southern farmer was asked if he had seen any of Lee's troops about that day. He growled out that he could give no information.

"How far is it to Buffalo River ?"

"Sir, I don't know."

"The devil you don't! How long have you lived here ?"

"All my life."

"Very well, sir, it is time you did know. Captain, put this gentleman in charge of a guard, and when we move walk him down to Buffalo River and show it to him."

That evening "this gentleman" tramped five miles away from home to look at a river which was as familiar to him as his own family.

PERSONAL JOTTINGS.

A gentleman who knew Sheridan well in his
fighting days gives the following pen-picture of
him :

"Sheridan looks the fighter in every one of his
scant inches, in every fiber of his sturdy frame, and
every feature of his florid face and compact, powerful looking head. Yet there was more than the mere
fighter look. The head and face wear an unmis-
takable expression of intellectual vigor. Sheridan
looks like a ruler of men : like the man who could,
as he did, make a scattered army cohere into a
victorious phalanx and throw it like an avalanche
on a flying foe. He is not more than five feet six
inches in height, while the breadth of his shoulders
and the depth of his chest are very great. His
hands and feet are small. The light ivory-handled
riding-whip, which is Sheridan's inseparable companion, was in his hand. Sheridan's face is unmistakably Irish in expression. It is slightly oval in
outline, well knit and compact in feature. The
lower jaw is long and powerful, coming down on
each side to a square, firm chin. The mouth,
draped by a mustache of moderate size, is a strong,
straight and rather mobile feature. The nose is one
of the fighting sort, small at the root, wide at the
nostrils and rather aquiline in form. The head of
'Cavalry Sheridan' is quite up to his reputation. It
is long, moderately high, quite broad, very compact,
with a good back head and base brain. The large pro-
portion of it is forward of the ears, though. You see

that this is a man of resources, not over confident, but quite self-possessed, firm to the last degree, with convictions which once taken last a lifetime. Sheridan's eyes are among the best, if not the very best, features of his remarkable face. These are of a warm, gray hue, which soften with a wonderful kindness or flash with a consuming fire. The wrath of this man must be terrific, while humor is, on the other hand, as much a part of his nature. The forehead is good, broad, not high, and the perceptives well developed and the eyebrows arched into the shape which is seen in antique sculpture, but so seldom visible in modern countenances.

"General Sheridan entered battle with a fixed resolve not to come out of it except as a conqueror, and the man who fights in this spirit is the least likely of all men to be injured. He fights with a resolution to win or die; and therefore fights, as the saying is, 'the very darndest that is in him.' He will win—at least the chances are ninety-nine to one in his favor—if the forces be anything like equal and the opposing commander not actuated by a similar resolve. In the courage of desperation there may be found a shield for its own rashness; and in proof thereof let us cite the fact that General Phil Sheridan has never received so much as a scratch during all the battles in which his personal daring has been so prominent."

MARCH, CAMP, AND FIELD.

A WAR CORRESPONDENT'S ESTIMATE AND RECOL-
LECTIONS OF GENERAL PHILIP SHERIDAN.

General Sheridan will undoubtedly be considered
a picturesque figure by future writers of American
history.   Occupying a subordinate position during
the first year of the civil war, he suddenly became
prominent as a dashing and successful cavalry
officer.   The opportunity for displaying his genius
came at last, and he instantly grasped it.   In the
West his fame was on a par with that of Sherman,
Thomas and Logan, and when Grant rose to the
rank of lieutenant-general and assumed the command of all the federal armies in the field, he brought
Sheridan with him to the East and assigned him to
the command of the cavalry corps in the Army of
the Potomac.   It was and always had been the
largest body of horsemen on either side of the
struggle.

On the Peninsula, in 1862, when McClellan made
his advance upon Richmond, the cavalry were dis-
tributed by divisions to the several infantry corps,
and though they made many important raids upon
the rear lines of the Confederates, they played no
important part in the general engagements of that
year.   Pleasonton and Kilpatrick and Dahlgren
and Torbert and Wilson were brave and intelligent
officers, but they did not possess that rare faculty
for handling twenty or thirty thousand horsemen
which Sheridan so signally displayed.

When the cavalry were consolidated by Hooker and placed as a separate corps under the command of Pleasonton their value as an aggressive weapon was increased. At the battle of Brandy Plains, between the Rappahannock River and Culpepper, Pleasonton defeated and crippled Jeb Stuart, and he inflicted great loss on Lee by the destruction of Confederate ammunition and supply trains during the second invasion of Pennsylvania. The cavalry also took a prominent part on the last day of Gettysburg.

SHERIDAN AS A TACTICIAN.

But it was reserved for Sheridan to show the military student that large masses of cavalry could be as successfully handled in battles for the possession of mountain passes and amid dense forests as they had been in the open field by Murat and other great European *sabreurs*.

The services rendered by Sheridan during the overland campaign of 1864 in forcing Lee to make frequent changes of front, and his thorough protection of Grant's flanks and lines of communication were sufficient to give him fame. Still it was reserved for him to show that, though a great cavalry leader, he could handle with equal facility large bodies of infantry.

Twice had Lee successfully called "check!" on the commanders of the Army of the Potomac by crossing over into Maryland and Pennsylvania, and though the battles of Antietam and Gettysburg greatly crippled him, the Confederate leader had for a time relieved Richmond from direct assault. Counting upon Washington bureau influences he made a third attempt in this direction during 1864, and drove Hunter out of the Shenandoah Valley. Instead of changing front and releasing his grip upon Richmond, Grant ordered Sheridan to the Valley with 12,000 sabers and the Sixth and Nineteenth Army corps, which, with General Crook's old Kanawha corps, gave him a complete army. The Shenandoah campaign forms one of the most brilliant episodes of the war, for when his hand was ready Sheridan fought Jubal Early at Winchester, which doubled him up, and subsequently almost annihilated him at Cedar Creek.

When the curtain was rung up for the last act in this tremendous war Sheridan came back to Grant's side at Petersburg, and he fought the battle of Five Forks so brilliantly that it practically ended the struggle.

Briefly told, this is the record of Sheridan, and it was natural that he should stand beside Grant and Sherman when a grateful people rewarded its servants.

IMPULSIVE BUT GENEROUS.

General Sheridan was one of those impulsive men who often create enemies without intent. To his officers he was stern and exacting, and, when excited, was apt to be harsh and inconsiderate in his treatment of subordinates. But in his cooler moments Sheridan would make amends, his apologies being all the sweeter because unexpected, and sometimes not deserved.

Courage and dash always won Sheridan's heart, and he held Wilson and Torbert and Custer, his division generals, in warm esteem. After a bold

movement his words of praise came like a hot torrent from his lips, causing the cheek of the recipient to flush and glow. With his men, the rank and file, "Little Phil," as they loved to call him, was kind and thoughtful. He took especial pains to see that they were well clothed and well fed, and while in the field he did not recklessly throw his troops upon the enemy, but keeping his forces in hand dealt terrible blows. When he put his men into battle he expected them to fight and compelled them to do so, never hesitating to share their dangers in leading them on in person.

A CHARACTERISTIC INCIDENT.

On one occasion a brigade commander failed in completely executing a movement in the general plan of an engagement. Perceiving the error at a glance, Sheridan galloped over and straightened the line, meanwhile hurling angry words upon the head of the unfortunate commander. Seeing that part of the movement in successful progress, Sheridan galloped away to another part of the field. The brigade, smarting under the reproof given their leader, performed prodigies of valor and covered themselves with glory. The following day Sheridan rode over to the brigade as it stood under arms. Raising his hat to the Brigadier, he shouted :

"Men of the Third brigade ! To your bravery we owe much of the success of yesterday. As soldiers, I thank you and your General, and shall hereafter know that I can always rely upon the old Third brigade."

Amid the wild cheers of the men "Little Phil"

disappeared, but there were no more devoted followers of Sheridan than this happy brigadier and his gratified command. The incident had a Napoleonic touch about it which reminded the writer of McClellan in his best days.

SEVERE BUT KIND.

General Sheridan, like all impulsive men, had an extremely kind heart. Stern in discipline, he was merciless in treating military crimes. One day he had just ordered a group of foragers to be severely punished, and was riding down a side road when he noticed a trooper lying on the grass under a fence.

"What's the matter, my man?" he asked, reining in his horse.

"I got wounded out on the picket line, General," replied the soldier, "and am trying to get to the hospital."

"Slow work on foot," remarked Sheridan. "Where's your horse?"

"Killed under me when I got hit," was the terse reply.

Directing some of his orderlies to dismount the General saw the wounded man placed on the saddle behind one of them and ordered him to convey his charge to the nearest surgeon. Many instances of this kind could be related.

HIS APPEARANCE IN BATTLE.

In action Sheridan was an extraordinary man. It was his habit to select a rising bit of ground, which enabled him to view the greater part of his lines. Sitting there in the saddle, like a carved statue, his eye would watch everything, and if a critical moment occurred he instantly galloped to the scene, and by his presence restored confidence among his men. It was a grand sight to see him ride swiftly along the lines just before a charge began, and raise the enthusiasm of his troops to fever heat. Then his cheek glowed with excitement, his eye grew bright and there was a magnetic influence about him which extended itself to every saber and musket bearer in the ranks. At such moments he seemed transformed, and it was no wonder that his troops afterward moved with steadiness and determination into the vortex of flame that awaited them.

At the battle of Winchester, when the old Sixth corps crossed the field in magnificent array to pierce Early's center and so carry the day, Sheridan rode along their flanks and cried out:

"Men of the Sixth, our victory to-day depends upon you!"

These electrical words passed from mouth to mouth, and animated by the confidence of their leader the men of the Roman cross carried their tattered colors forward and clean through the Confederate center. Then Early was "sent whirling through Winchester," as Sheridan epigrammatically expressed it in his despatches.

SHERIDAN AND WRIGHT.

At Cedar Creek, when he made his historic ride from Winchester, Sheridan found the lines reforming under Wright for another assault. Satisfying himself that the lines of battle were correct, he dashed along the front of his army and encouraged his men by his visible presence. Then he sent them forward, and by one fell stroke ended the Shenandoah campaign.

WHAT CONSTITUTES A GREAT GENERAL.

Two qualities are necessary to make a great general. He must know not only how to fight, but when to fight, and he should always aim at producing permanent results. In our civil war many really good commanders could fight when the occasion arose, but they often fought without preparation or not at the proper moment. Besides, they were content to win the battle without following it up and with another blow emphasize the first by permanently disabling their antagonist. McClellan, having defeated Lee at Antietam, was content to let the Army of Northern Virginia slip through his fingers and escape across the Potomac to recuperate. At Gettysburg Meade was satisfied with whipping Lee on Culp's Hill, and permitted the Confederate leader to make good his retreat into the Shenandoah Valley.

Sheridan, like Grant and Sherman, was made of different stuff, for when he entered the valley he made up his mind to render that convenient field of operations forever useless to the Confederacy.

When Grant was preparing for his overland campaign he recruited the Army of the Potomac by emptying the fortifications around Washington. This was contrary to the ideas of Secretary Stanton, who insisted that the national capital must be guarded against the flank attacks of Lee.

"Once I get started," replied Grant, "there will

be no flank movements, for I will keep Lee too busy."

SHERIDAN'S PERMANENT BLOWS.

This was Grant's plan, and it was also Sherman's, so when Sheridan found himself on an independent line he decided to inflict a crushing blow. A good deal of harsh criticism has been made on Sheridan's devastation of the Shenandoah Valley as unnecessary and cruel. But, as Sherman has very aptly said, "War is always cruel," and in this case Sheridan's cruelty was in reality kindness.

He advanced up the valley in August, 1864, very leisurely, allowing Early to fall back as leisurely. His object was twofold. He wanted to examine the topography of the valley and allow the luxuriant wheat crop to ripen. Having accomplished this, he gave Early time to reap and stack the wheat, and then in September descended upon his lines like a whirlwind. He thrashed Early soundly and destroyed the garnered wheat by fire, and in some instances destroyed barns and buildings. By smashing Early he weakened Lee, and by destroying the wheat crop deprived the Confederate leader of his anticipated supplies.

These were permanent results. The Shenandoah was closed as a line for menacing operations, and Sheridan's campaign narrowed the boundaries for both Lee and Johnston. The battles of Winchester and Cedar Creek were brilliant victories, but they were chiefly valuable because their effects were felt long after the smoke of cannon and musket had disappeared. As a strategic movement, his valley campaign stands on a par with Sherman's march to the sea and Grant's line of circumvallation around Lee. The three fitted together and ended the war.

Regarding the charge of cruelty in devastating the valley, it need only be said that Napoleon did likewise, and so did Wellington, and so did Frederick the Great. Real generals are like surgeons, for they must not shrink from giving pain if they wish to make their operations successful. McClellan sought to save the lives of his soldiers by besieging an inferior force at Yorktown, and lost more men by disease than he could have sacrificed by direct assault.

That was what made Sheridan a great general.

A true soldier, a born tactician, and a man who knew just when to fight, Sheridan won imperishable renown, and his name will forever shine brightly on the pages of American history. Though richly rewarded by his country, he deserved it by faithful service and the display of high military genius.

SHERIDAN'S DETERMINATION.

In speaking one day of Sheridan General Grant said: "When Sheridan arrived from his raid around Lee I gave him his orders. They were to move on the left and attack Lee. If the movement succeeded he was to advance; if it failed he was to make his way into North Carolina and join Sherman. When Sheridan read this part he was, I saw, disappointed. His countenance fell. He had just made a long march, a severe march, and now the idea of another march into North Carolina would disconcert any commander—even Sheridan. He, however, said nothing. I said:

" 'Sheridan, although I have provided for your
retreat into North Carolina in the event of failure,
I have no idea that you will fail, no idea that you
will go to Carolina. I mean to end this business
right here.'

"Sheridan's eyes lit up, and he said with enthusiasm :

" 'That's the talk. Let us end the business
here.'

"But, of course, I had to think of the loyal
North, and if we failed in striking Lee it would
have satisfied the North for Sheridan to go to the
Carolinas. The movement, however, succeeded, for
my next news from Sheridan was the battle of Five
Forks, one of the finest battles in the war."

"There was no time in the war," said General
Grant on another day, "when it was more critical
than after the battle of Five Forks, when Lee abandoned Richmond. Sheridan led the pursuit of Lee.
He went after him almost with the force of volition,
and the country owes him a great debt of gratitude
for the manner in which he attacked that retreat.
It was one of the incomparable things in the war.

" The pursuing army was in three parts, under
Generals Meade, Ord and Sheridan. I was with
Ord's command. One day I got word from Sheridan saying that it was most important that I should
go at once to his headquarters, as Meade had given
his part of the army orders to move in such a manner that Lee might break through and escape. I
reached Sheridan at midnight. He was very anxious. Meade had given him orders to move on the
right flank and cover Richmond. This Sheridan

thought would open the door for Lee to escape toward Johnston. Meade's fear was that by uncovering Richmond Lee would get into our rear and trouble our communications. Sheridan's idea was to move on the left flank, swing between Lee and the road to Johnston, leave Richmond and our rear to take care of themselves and press Lee and attack him wherever he could be found. Meade's view was that of an engineer. His theory secured the safety of our army, the safety of Richmond and all the triumphs of the campaign, but at the same time it left the door open for Lee.

AT SAILOR CREEK.

"My judgment coincided with Sheridan's. The question was not the occupation of Richmond, but the destruction of the army. I told Meade that Richmond was only a collection of houses, while Lee was an active force injuring the country. I did not want Richmond so much as I wanted Lee. I changed Meade's orders, and he went to work in the most loyal manner. The movement threw us between Lee and the Carolinas. The next morning, when Meade's force came up, Sheridan attacked Lee. This is known as the battle of Sailor Creek. When I came on the field and found what a rout he had made of the Confederates and that prisoners were coming in by shoals, I saw there was no more fighting left in that army, and the responsibility of any further destruction of life must be on their shoulders, not mine, and I resolved to write to Lee, asking for his surrender."

STONE RIVER.

"Speaking of Rosecrans' army," said General

Grant, "Sheridan's command at the battle of Stone River was, from all I can learn about it, a wonderful bit of fighting. It showed what a great general can do even when in a subordinate command, for I believe Sheridan in that battle saved Rosecrans' army.

"Mission Ridge," remarked General Grant, "although a great victory, would have ended in the destruction of Bragg but for our mistake in not knowing the ground. Sheridan showed his genius in that battle, and to him I owe the capture of most of the prisoners that were taken. Although commanding a division only, he saw in the crisis of the engagement that it was necessary to advance beyond the point indicated in his orders. He saw that I could not know on account of my ignorance of the ground, and with the instinct of military genius pushed ahead. If others had followed his example we should have had Bragg's army."

HOW SHERIDAN ENDED THE WAR.

THE UNFLAGGING PURSUIT OF LEE WHICH TERMINATED IN VICTORY AT APPOMATTOX.

In his volume "With General Sheridan in Lee's Last Campaign," Colonel F. H. Newhall, a staff officer, tells in the chapter entitled "The Pursuit of Lee" how Sheridan ended the war.

"On April 8, 1865, General Sheridan sent a dispatch to General Grant reporting his move on Appomattox Depot and saying: "We will perhaps

finish the job in the morning. I do not think Lee
means to surrender until compelled to."

"As Lee was compelled to surrender next morning, this is the last dispatch General Sheridan found
it necessary to write. All through the campaign
he had been urging on the whole army by word and
example, and now he was to see his hopes realized.
From the morning that we saw him riding out of
his camp below Petersburg until this hour he had
never doubted for a moment that a crowning victory
would attend our arms should the whole force be
put vigorously in and the opening success thoroughly followed up. Looking back at what he
wrote to General Grant, we may see how from the
first he did not hesitate to commit himself to the
defeat and capture of Lee, and how he boldly
avowed his belief in entire success, shouldering, as
it were, the responsibility of the undertaking, and
rendering himself liable to the severest criticism if
failure had ensued.

"As early as the 31st of March, in the mud at
Dinwiddie Court House, he wrote: 'If the ground
would permit, I believe I could, with the Sixth corps,
turn the enemy's left flank (at Five Forks) or cut
up their lines,' and we have seen how he made good
this declaration with the Fifth corps the next day,
and when this was done how he promptly moved
against the flank of Lee's main line at Petersburg
without waiting for orders. From the Namozine
road, on April 4, two days before the decisive battle
of Sailors' Creek, he wrote: 'If we press on we
will no doubt get the whole army.' "

"At Jetersville the next afternoon he said in his

dispatch (to Grant): 'I wish you were here yourself. I feel confident of capturing the Army of Northern Virginia if we exert ourselves. I see no escape for Lee.' Then, as the enemy staggered back from the blow he dealt them at Sailors' Creek, Sheridan wrote, 'If the thing is pressed I think Lee will surrender.'

"At sunrise and at dark that day he had three times renewed these confident and urgent messages. 'I will move on Appomattox Court House. Should we not intercept the enemy and he be forced into Lynchburg surrender there is beyond question.'

"If it is possible push on your troops. We may have handsome results in the morning.'

"'If General Gibbon and the Fifth Army corps can get up to-night we will perhaps finish the job in the morning. I do not think Lee means to surrender until compelled to do so.'

LEE NOT READY TO YIELD.

"On the day before General Lee had written to General Grant, 'To be frank, I do not consider that the emergency has arisen to call for the surrender of this army.' If it had not arisen it was because of the open road to Danville.

"Although General Sheridan knew very well that the remnant of Lee's army confronted him on the road to Appomattox Court House and would try to break through to the railroad at sunrise, he never thought of abandoning his position there, even if the infantry (General Gibbon and Fifth corps) could not get up. As it was, it pattered by our headquarters at daybreak on April 9, 1865, and

with it came General Ord, who would control the
infantry. General Sheridan started to look after
the cavalry, who were already skirmishing briskly
with the advancing enemy. Their infantry outnumbered the cavalry and they knew they were
fighting for a point that must be gained or all
would be lost. They must prevent the closing of
the Danville road.

"For a little while the cavalry held their ground
under General Crook, but when Sheridan came up
he sent word to Generals Ord and Griffin to hurry
on and ordered Crook to fall back slowly and not
sacrifice his men by trying to check the heavy
force attacking him.

"General Merritt was now ordered to get his
divisions mounted and move round the right of
our infantry line, and Crook, as he retired, was
instructed to give way in the same direction. Gibbon, with the Twenty-fourth corps; Griffin, with
the Fifth and a division of colored troops belonging
to General Ord's command, were ensconced among
the trees silently waiting for orders to advance. On
the extreme left General Davies was skirmishing
with some rebel cavalry, and Mackenzie was out
there somewhere stealing round to their flank.
Apparently we were deserting the field as if we had
accepted the situation and would now permit General Lee to pass on unmolested.

"Seeing our troopers march off by the flank,
apparently giving up the fight for the road and
opening a way of retreat, Lee's men yelled and
quickened their pace and doubled their fire. They
would get away after all, they thought, for Sheri-

dan's cavalry alone couldn't hope to stop them, and evidently we had no other troops at hand.

ONE ROAD OF ESCAPE.

"Appomattox Depot gained, their troubles would be at an end, for thence the road to Danville is straight; at last they would have cast us behind them and we might catch them if we could. Fast walkers they, and not much encumbered with *impedimenta*, they could laugh at our heavily loaded infantry, and if they should ever join Johnston—well, wonderful things would happen then; so they gave us their best yell and pressed on faster. But not far; for the sound of their peculiar cheer had hardly entered the woods before the long line of our infantry emerged and burst upon their astonished sight. They staggered back and their whole line wavered as if each particular man was terror-struck. They didn't even fire, palsied as they were by surprise, but rolled back like a receding wave. Then our troops advanced, saving their cheers for the end of the Rebellion, which everybody felt must soon be reached.

"The undulating lines of the infantry, now rising the crest of a knoll, now dipping into a valley or ravine, pressed on grandly across the open, for here, at last, we were out of the woods in the beautiful, clear fields, and if the Rebellion should crumble here all who fought against it might see it fall. The cavalry on the right trotted out in advance of the infantry line and made ready to take the enemy in flank if he should stand to fight or dash at his train, which now were in full view beyond Appo-

mattox Court House. At the head of the horsemen rode Custer, of the golden locks, the broad
sombrero turned up from his broad, bronzed face,
the ends of his crimson cravat floating over his
shoulders, gold galore spangling his jacket-sleeves,
a pistol in his boot, jangling spurs on his heels and
a ponderous claymore swinging at his side—a wild
daredevil of a general and a prince of advance
guards, quick to see and to act.

THE SURRENDER.

" As he is about to strike a final blow for the good
cause, his hand is stayed and his great sword drops
back again into the scabbard, for out from the
enemy's lines comes a rider 'bound on bound,'
bearing a white flag of truce to ask time to consummate surrender.

" General Sheridan is just behind and word is sent
to him at once. The wild cheers of the men have
passed the good news to him and he meets the messenger half-way. The General notifies General Ord,
and the whole line is halted in the crest overlooking
Appomattox Court House and the valley beyond,
in which lies the broken army of Northern Virginia.

" General Sheridan, confiding in the flag of truce,
rode out in front of his cavalry and struck across
toward Appomattox Court House, which was about
the center of the position our troops held at halting.
He had hardly gone a hundred yards when some
rebel troops in front of him suddenly fired on his
little party. Luckily they aimed badly and nobody
was hurt, and the General and his staff, supposing
some mistake was at the bottom of this eccentric

proceeding, waved their caps and made other friendly signals only to be answered by another volley, happily as ineffectual as the first. Then galloping away they found shelter behind a hill, and Major Allen, of our staff, rode rapidly into the enemy's lines, on the flank of this dangerous party, and demanded to know the cause of this violation of the flag. A general in command, who evidently supposed himself to be General Taylor in Mexico, replied that South Carolinians never surrendered, and declined to receive any order to suspend hostilities. Custer hearing this firing promptly moved out to look into it. Meanwhile, Generals Sheridan wended his way to the Court House, where he was met by the Confederate Generals Gordon and Wilcox on neutral ground. Just as they began to talk firing was heard again where the South Carolinians were. General Gordon ordered a staff officer to find out what it meant.

"'Never mind,' said Sheridan. 'I know what it is. Let them fight it out.'

"In a moment all was quiet, and the last angry shot had been fired from the war-worn lines, which now awaited the result of the negotiations for surrender.

"General Sheridan said he was anxious to avoid further loss of life, but he must have some assurance that the proposition to surrender was *bona fide* and not a makeshift to gain time and advantage. He sent the dispatch of General Lee asking for an interview to General Grant, who was met by the messenger, five or six miles away on the main road, hurrying to meet Sheridan.

" As Grant rode up to the Court House Generals Ord and Sheridan met him.

" ' How are you, Sheridan ? ' said Grant on dismounting. To which in a quiet manner Sheridan replied :

" ' First rate, thank you ; how are you ? '

" ' Is General Lee up there ? '

" ' Yes.'

" ' Well, then, we'll go up.'

Phil Sheridan had ended the war.

SHERIDAN'S LETTERS ABOUT WINCHESTER.

Col. Herbert E. Hill, of the Eighth Vermont, who has published magazine articles on the campaign in the Shenandoah Valley, received the following autograph letters from Gen. Sheridan corroborating his statements :

CHICAGO, Oct. 17, 1887.

COL. HERBERT E. HILL, Boston, Mass.:

Between 6 and 7 o'clock on Monday, Oct. 19, the officer on picket at Winchester reported to me, while I was in bed at the house of Col. Edwards, the commanding officer, the sound of scattering artillery shots. These I supposed to be made by Grover's division of the Nineteenth Corps, which was to have made a reconnaissance that morning. My black horse Winchester was saddled, as well as the horses of my staff officers, and we started about 8 o'clock, passing through the main street of Winchester.

On reaching the southern suburbs of the town the

sound of artillery indicated a battle to me unmistakably. We walked leisurely until we reached Mill Creek, half a mile or so from the town, trying to determine by the sound whether the firing was coming towards us or receding, and after crossing Mill Creek and rising a little bluff on the south side, we saw the heads of the troops retreating coming rapidly to the rear. I at once ordered a halt, directed that the train be stopped and parked at Mill Creek, and sent orders that the brigade in garrison at Winchester be stretched across the country and all stragglers stopped. Then, taking twenty men from the escort I rode rapidly on, as nearly parallel to the valley pike as the crowd of stragglers would permit, until I struck Getty's division of the Sixth Corps, three-quarters of a mile north of Middletown, reaching there a little before 10 o'clock A.M. I rode my black horse Winchester until just before the final attack at 4 o'clock in the afternoon, when I changed to my gray horse, which I rode until the battle was over.

P. H. SHERIDAN,
Lieutenant-General United States Army.

CHICAGO, Oct. 18, 1887.

COL. HERBERT E. HILL, Boston, Mass.:

The enemy captured from our troops in the morning twenty-four pieces of artillery. These were recaptured, and twenty-four more from the enemy in the afternoon, making forty-eight pieces. Ten battle-flags were also captured from the enemy. The black horse Winchester died Oct. 2, 1878, and is set up on exhibition at the Military Institute,

Governor's Island.　The gray horse was burned up in the Chicago fire, Oct. 9, 1871.

P. H. SHERIDAN,
Lieutenant-General United States Army.

———

SHERIDAN'S LAST VISIT TO WEST POINT.

In speaking of Sheridan, one of the Congressional Board of Visitors to West Point relates the following :

General Sheridan, hale and hearty, was moving about over the smooth green sward and well-kept drives at West Point amid all the glory of booming cannon and rows of polished steel with which a military post welcomes a general commanding.　As Sheridan stood before the semi-circle of slender, erect young cadets to hand over to them the pile of diplomas which summed up their four years of hard work and exacting drill, his thoughts evidently went back to the time when he, too, stood upon the threshold of his military career with nothing but his second lieutenant's commission and his academic training.　In the unassuming little speech which he made to the cadets before the superintendent began to call up the graduates to receive their diplomas from the General's hands, Sheridan laid bare the secret of his own military success.

"Gentlemen," said he, "I'll tell you how it all came about.　It was all due to two things.　When I went out from under the shadow of these trees, as you are doing to-day, I resolved that I would make

myself the best second lieutenant in ..e army.
Whatever I took up, even if it were the simplest of
duties, I tried to do it better than it had ever been
done before by others. No matter if you are hidden
in an obscure post, never content yourself with
doing your second best, however unimportant the
occasion. In the second place, I always looked out
for the common soldier. Make the men in the
ranks feel that you are devoting days of care and
thought to their comfort and safety. Trust your
reputation to the private, let him speak for you,
and in the battle and on the march he will never
let your military fame suffer by his cowardice or
negligence. Keep these two things in view, and,
with your West Point training, success is assured
to you."

SHERIDAN'S RIDE.

BY THOMAS BUCHANAN READ.

Up from the South at break of day,
Bringing to Winchester fresh dismay,
The affrighted air with a shudder bore,
Like a herald in haste to the chieftain's door,
The terrible grumble and rumble and roar,
Telling the battle was on once more,
And Sheridan twenty miles away!

And wider still those billows of war
Thundered along the horizon's bar,
And louder yet into Winchester rolled
The roar of that red sea uncontrolled,
Making the blood of the listener cold
As he thought of the stake in that fiery fray,
And Sheridan twenty miles away!

But there is a road from Winchester town
A good, broad highway leading down;
And there through the flush of the morning light
A steed as black as the steeds of night
Was seen to pass with eagle flight.
As if he knew the terrible need,
He stretched away with his utmost speed;
Hill rose and fell, but his heart was gay
With Sheridan fifteen miles away!

Still sprang from those swift hoofs thundering south,
The dust like smoke from the cannon's mouth.
Or the trail of a comet sweeping faster and faster,
Foreboding to traitors the doom of disaster;
The heart of the steed and the heart of the master
Were beating like prisoners assaulting their walls,
Impatient to be where the battle-field calls ;
Every nerve of the charger was strained to full play
With Sheridan only ten miles away!

Under his spurning feet the road
Like an arrowy Alpine river flowed,
And the landscape sped away behind
Like an ocean flying before the wind;
And the steed like a bark fed with furnace ire
Swept on with his wild eyes full of fire.
But lo! he is nearing his heart's desire,
He is snuffing the smoke of the burning fray,
With Sheridan only five miles away!

The first that the General saw were the groups
Of stragglers; and then the retreating troops.
What was done—what to do? a glance told him both;
Then striking his spurs with a terrible oath,
He dashed down the line 'mid a shower of huzzas,
And the wave of retreat checked its course there, because
The sight of the master compelled it to pause.
With foam and with dust the black charger was gray,
By the flash of his eye and his red nostril's play,

He seemed to the whole great army to say,
"I've brought you Sheridan, all the way
From Winchester town to save the day."

Hurrah, hurrah, for Sheridan!
Hurrah, hurrah, for horse and man!
And when their statues are placed on high,
Under the dome of the Union sky,
The American soldier's temple of fame—
There with the glorious General's name
Be it said in letters both bold and bright,
"Here is the steed that saved the day
By carrying Sheridan into the fight,
From Winchester, twenty miles away."

THE END.

MAGNET HANDBOOKS.

PRICE TWENTY-FIVE CENTS EACH.

BOOK OF USEFUL RECEIPTS, and Manufacturers' Guide.—By Professor JOHNSON.—For conciseness, reliability, and cheapness, this work is superior to any published. Not only does it contain a vast number of reliable and practical recipes and processes relating to the fine arts, trades, and general manufactures, but it gives full and explicit instructions for acquiring and successfully practising numerous arts and professions, such as Electrotyping and Electroplating, making and working an Electric Telegraph, Monochromatic and Crayon Painting, Vitremaine, and many others of equal value and importance.

A SCIENTIFIC TREATISE ON Stammering and Stuttering, and its cure.—We have here this difficult subject treated so intelligently and plainly that any person interested can read and learn the causes of the peculiar and distressing impediments in his speech. It thoroughly explains the different causes that produce stammering, and then proceeds to make plain the means of cure, so that any person with a determination to succeed, by following the instructions given, can cure himself of this most unhappy affliction, and at no expense but the cost of the book.

THE REAL SECRET ART AND Philosophy of Wooing, Winning, and Wedding.—Showing how maidens may become happy wives, and bachelors become happy husbands, in a brief space of time and by easy methods. Also containing complete directions for declaring intentions, accepting vows, and retaining affections, both before and after marriage.

CHOICE VERSES FOR VALENtines, Albums, and Wedding Celebrations.—Containing original and selected verses applicable to wooden, tin, silver, golden, and diamond wedding anniversaries; bouquet and birthday presentations, autograph-album verses and acrostics, and a variety of verses and poems adapted to social anniversaries and rejoicings.

THE AMERICAN REFERENCEBOOK.—A manual of facts, containing a chronological history of the United States; the public lands; everything about the constitution, debts, revenues, productions, wealth, population, railroads, exemption, interest, insolvent and assignment statutes of the United States, &c.

KEY TO COMPOSITION: or, How to Write a Book.—A complete guide to authorship, and practical instructor in all kinds of literary labor. As an aid and instructor to those who desire to follow literary pursuits permanently for profit, or to those who write for recreation and leasure, this book is indispensable.

GYMNASTICS WITHOUT A TEACHER.—This book plainly explains to you how to go about learning all the rougher branches of gymnastics. Every man and boy ought to learn the different exercises described in this book, if he wishes to live a healthy life, and preserve a sound and vigorous body, a sharp eye, and supple limbs.

FORTUNE-TELLING MADE EASY or, the Dreamer's Sure Guide.—This book will tell you about your destiny, your prospective marriage, your business prospects, your love-affairs. The book is a perfect oracle of fate.

FRENCH IN A FORTNIGHT, without a master.—A royal road to a knowledge of the Parisian tongue, in fifteen easy lessons on accent, grammar, and pronunciation.

INCIDENTS OF AMERICAN CAMP-LIFE.—A collection of tragic, pathetic, and humorous events, which actually occurred during the late civil war.

OUR KNOWLEDGE-BOX; or, old secrets and new discoveries.

THE YOUNG WIFE'S OWN COOK-BOOK.—This very valuable manual teaches plainly how to buy, dress, cook, serve, and carve every kind of fish, fowl, meat, game, and vegetable. Also, how to preserve fruits and vegetables, and how to make pastry.

THE FAMILY CYCLOPEDIA.—A complete and practical domestic manual for all classes. This valuable and comprehensive work is needed in every house.

THE ART OF SELF-DEFENSE; or, Boxing without a Master.—With forty large illustrations, showing all the different positions, blows, stops, and guards. By NED DONNELLY, Professor of Boxing to the London Athletic Club.

THE ART OF BEAUTIFYING AND Preserving the Hair; or, How to Make the Hair Grow.—This is the only exhaustive scientific work on the hair published.

HAWTHORNE'S COMIC AND TRAGIC DIALOGUES.—Including many of the most affecting, amusing, and spirited dialogues ever written,—affording opportunities for the display of every different quality of action, voice, and delivery,—suitable for schools, academies, anniversaries, and parlor presentations.

HAWTHORNE'S JUVENILE SPEAKER AND READER.—Prepared expressly and carefully for the use of young children. Containing a large number of pieces, some simple enough to please infants, while all are sure to delight and improve children of every age.

HAWTHORNE'S TRAGIC RECITER.—Containing the very best pieces ever written expressive of Love, Hate, Fear, Rage, Revenge, Jealousy, and the other most melting, stirring, and startling passions of the human heart.

HAWTHORNE'S COMIC RECITER. Filled with the liveliest, jolliest, laughter-provoking stories, lectures, and other humorous pieces.

Hawthorne's Book of Readymade Speeches on all subjects that can occur, whether on serious, sentimental, or humorous occasions. Including speeches and replies at dinners, receptions, festivals, political meetings, military reviews, firemen's gatherings, and indeed wherever and whenever any party, large or small, is gathered to dine, to mourn, to congratulate, or to rejoice. Appended to which are forms of all kinds of resolutions, &c., with a great number of sentiments and toasts.

Theatricals at Home; or, Plays for the Parlor. Plainly teaching how to dress, make up, study, and perform at private theatrical parties. To which are added how to arrange and display tableaux vivants, shadow pantomimes, drawing-room magic, acting charades, conundrums, enigmas, &c., with explanatory engravings.

Snip, Snap, Snorum, and nearly one hundred other parlor games, such as juvenile card-games, games of forfeits, games of action, games with pen and pencil. Including many new and all the old favorite amusements calculated to make home happy and set the youngsters screaming wild with innocent delight.

The Art of Canning, Pickling, and smoking the various kinds of Meat, Fish, and Game. Also, how to preserve and keep, fresh and full of flavor, fruits, berries, and vegetables. To which is added complete directions for making candies and choice confections.

Fishing with Hook and Line.—This book gives plain and full directions for catching all the different kinds of fish found in American waters; the proper season for fishing for them, and the bait, tackle, &c., to be used.

Honest Abe's Jokes.—A collection of authentic jokes and squibs of Abraham Lincoln.

www.ingramcontent.com/pod-product-compliance
Lightning Source LLC
Chambersburg PA
CBHW022354020726
47500CB00002B/277